THE CHAINED IMMORTAL

THE CHAINED IMMORTAL

The Doomsayer Journeys Book 2

STEVE WETHERELL

"And I looked unto the skies, and I saweth a cloud, and the cloud did look suspiciously like a frog, but with hair, and verily I knew that the end was upon us, for are not hairy frogs traditionally regarded as harbingers of despair? No? Well who asked you? Nobody, that's who. Get out."

-From the Chronicles of Celia Doom

1

Hope and the Lack Thereof

The planet Bersch. Named long ago by an egotistical and opportunistic astronomer. Home of a hodgepodge of sentient beings, some of them more and some of them less than human. Also the home of the Clarions, an ancient race sent to guide and protect those less developed than themselves, but unfortunately stranded for the last thousand years after a remarkable set of coincidences saw them crash land on Bersch's northernmost continent.

Bersch spins in the orbit of its sun as it always has, unaware that somewhere in the inky folds of space a ball of nuclear refuse is heading toward it with all the easy grace of a cataclysm.

Only a select few know that in less than a year pretty much everything is going to explode. Unfortunately, these are the same people who have been stranded on the Ice Plains for the better part of a millennium. Near the village of Kaneq—a settlement protected from the elements by an invisible wall of heat—lies a building long since buried under tons of snow. It is the *Sentinel*, a star-faring ship of the Clarions, now a tomb for ancient knowledge and baffling relics known to the locals simply as the Dome. The elders and councilmen of Kaneq meet there now, because the first thing any sensible species does in the presence of disaster is form a committee.

Dunman, Kaneq's mayor, wrung his hands nervously and smoothed down his already smooth hair. He had been doing this a lot more than usual lately and was starting to wear a bald patch on his scalp. "It's not that I don't have faith in the boy, Truggle," he said. "It's just that I for one would feel a lot safer if we had a contingency plan."

Truggle, eldest of the elders, peered out through the fog of his pipe smoke. "And is this how the rest of you feel?" he said.

The elders and higher council of Kaneq were gathered around a table in the bowels of the Dome. The weekly meeting was more urgent and uncomfortable than usual.

Tenbon, a senior elder, cleared her throat. "Sorry, Truggle, it's just that there are better men I can think of than Bip to pin the fate of the world on. He's not the man his father was."

Truggle puffed mechanically at his pipe. "I remind you, he has been trained by the best," he said.

All eyes in the room turned to Rynford and Glimton.

"Don't look at me," said Glimton. "I told you all he was a talentless pleb from the start."

"And you, Rynford?" said Truggle. Rynford scratched uncomfortably at his muscular neck. "I've trained better hunters..." he conceded.

"You see?" said Dunman.

"Pah!" said Truggle. "It's nice to see how much faith in my judgement you lot really have."

Tenbon sighed. "It's true that we don't all share your faith in Bip, Truggle," she said. "But can you blame us? This is our last chance, our last volunteer. The astral disaster strikes in less than a year, and we barely have time to select more volunteers as it is!"

"Then what do you suggest?" said Truggle.

Tenbon looked around at the other elders. "We thought that maybe a large party of volunteers, all the young men and women of the village, would stand a better chance."

Truggle puffed on his pipe, looking accusingly around the room. "You'd risk the lives of an entire generation?"

"Dammit, Truggle! We're talking about the end of the world, here!

The destruction of the planet! I'd sacrifice the entire village if I had to!"

The room was silent. Truggle looked slowly from face to face. "Give me time, ladies and gentlemen. Have a little faith in me, won't you?"

Various people in the room shifted uncomfortably, unsure of where to place their loyalties.

Dunman spoke up. "But what makes you so sure that the Plunkerton boy is the man for the job, Truggle?"

"Instinct. Wisdom."

Tenbon clucked her tongue. "Thin hooks to hang the fate of a world on, my friend."

Truggle looked sadly about the room. "Then, elders, council members, I am afraid I have no choice but to dismiss myself from this meeting. Good day."

Using the broom he always carried, Truggle rowed himself out of the room on his rickety wheelchair. The remaining people looked uncomfortably at the walls and ceiling, avoiding one another's eyes. After a while, Rynford let out a frustrated sigh, slapped his massive hands on the table and left the room.

"Anyone else?" said Tenbon. No one moved.

TRUGGLE ROWED himself far into the deepest corridors of the Dome, down into sectors that had been long forgotten or long since abandoned. The axels of his wheelchair squeaked eerily in the gloom. He reached a seemingly blank wall and tapped it in three distinct places with his broom. A large panel slid aside to reveal a row of numbers counting steadily downward, blinking energetically in the stillness of the lower levels.

"Instinct. Wisdom." The old man grinned mirthlessly.

THE CITY OF PANTHALUS, though the farthest settlement from the Empire's cultural heart of Argustin, was known throughout Regalious for its stunning architecture. Traveling down the long, straight road, through the flat farmlands that surrounded it, the city seemed like some dreamer's hobby model rather than a place where people lived. It stood atop a grassy hill, white and shining and crowned by a great palace that stood like an oversized stone set in an already beautiful ring. Flags of all colors flapped lazily in the gentle morning air.

In the clear sunshine, Panthalus gleamed like a fairytale.

Of course, the reality of the fair city was far grimmer on closer inspection. High taxes for city beatification meant people had to work long and hard—and those who could not keep up were often forced onto the streets. Also, surrounded by farmland as it was, living space in Panthalus was scarce enough without residential areas being cleared out for botanical gardens and huge, ornate reflecting pools. Hence, in the alleyways and byways of the clean, white city, hiding behind Panthalus's thin veil of beauty, a whole subculture of derelicts and unfortunates massed like woodworm.

Those who could afford to live well in Panthalus lived very well indeed. Those who couldn't froze quietly in the winter, huddled under floral clocks and marble arches.

Of course Bip, like most tourists, was oblivious to this as he entered the massive and beautifully wrought city gates. So distracted was he by the towering, gleaming buildings and the careful mosaic of the paving slabs that he didn't notice the beggars being ushered violently from the streets and the jaded look of the shattered workers making their way to and from their homes. Bip spent most of his time with his neck craned upward as he traveled on the horse-drawn tram around the city, marveling at the various works of art that punctuated the streets.

The place was very different from Port Town. Though the crowds were of similar magnitude, the hubbub therein wasn't reinforced by the shouts of merchants and the screaming laughter of whores. In fact, the noise of Panthalus was a polite murmur in comparison to the aural brawl of Port Town.

The level of technological advancement was also significantly different from what Bip had seen in the Free Countries. In Panthalus, it was not uncommon to see horseless trams, driven by internal engines that ran on fuel, chugging along and spewing smoke rhythmically into the air. Bip had heard about such things but never seen one before. In Port Town, the only engine-powered devices had been the Imperially-controlled airboats.

One thing that particularly drew Bip's attention was the number of statues erected in the city. Not that the number of statues was unexpected in the heavily-decorated province—what was unusual was that all of the statues seemed to be of the same figure. From the oldest bronze castings to the newest marble renditions, the same crowned figure stood throughout the city, sometimes looking speculatively over the horizon, sometimes flourishing a mighty sword, sometimes crouched in deep thought. Leaning over, Bip tapped the tram driver on the shoulder. The driver, a thickset man with a heavily oiled moustache, turned around, shaken from whatever daydream was occupying his mind.

"Can I help, sir?" he said.

"Yes, actually," said Bip. "I was just wondering who the statue chap was. You know, the chap in all the statues?"

The driver looked around as they passed yet another towering likeness of the much-rendered figure. "Why, that's Emperor Draegul, sir," he said.

"What, all of them?" said Bip, frowning.

"Oh, yes," said the driver. "And no. They're not all the same person, but they are all Emperor Draegul, you see." The driver pointed at a few distant statues. "That there is Emperor Draegul the Seventh—they called him Draegul the Incredibly Fair and Kind. And that one there is Draegul the Fourth, Draegul the Most Generous and Not At All Evil in Any Way Whatsoever."

Bip squinted through his glasses at the statues. They all looked more or less identical, bar their differing poses.

"There's a strong family resemblance," said the driver, guessing at Bip's confusion.

"So is there a Draegul on the throne today?" said Bip.

"Oh, yes," said the driver. "Emperor Tomberry Torrid Draegul the Tenth—Draegul the Really Nice Guy Once You Get to Know Him."

Bip looked up at another of the statues, this one holding the hand of a weeping child. "This Emperor Draegul, he must be a very popular man?" asked Bip.

The driver turned to look at him, a look of mistrustful cynicism in his eye. "Oh, yes," he said. "Extremely popular. Very popular indeed." The driver turned back to the road ahead, muttering something that sounded a bit like "bloody tourists," though Bip couldn't be sure.

Suddenly, something else about the streets of Panthalus caught Bip's eye—that of the presence of the Imperial Regulators, their gray top hats bobbing through the crowds like so many shark fins. Bip had a stomach-churning moment of paranoia. Something told him that thieves weren't welcome in Panthalus, and he didn't think it wholly improbable that his and Azron's descriptions had been passed on from the Free Countries via telegram. And even if that wasn't the case, Bip thought it safer to find a place where there were as few of the lurking enforcers around as possible.

Once again, he wished that Azron hadn't decided to go his own way. The lanky thief had always seemed to know what to do in these kinds of situations. Thinking quickly, Bip hopped off the tram as it slowed for a corner and stumbled into an alleyway discreetly disguised by carefully grown wallflowers. It was there that he found his first clue to the harsher underlying reality of life in Panthalus. The alleyway, as with all alleyways across the ultraverse, smelt strongly of urine.

Bip continued to follow the foul-smelling passageway as it twisted into a network of smaller roads and underpasses. There were no works of art here, no statues, and no fountains. There was just dankness, the sound of faraway coughing the only thing breaking the thick, wet silence. Occasionally Bip would run afoul of other people traveling the alleyways. These people didn't have the well-scrubbed appearance of the citizens in the city squares. They were dirtier, harder-looking people who glared suspiciously as he passed.

Walking for some immeasurable period of time, he began to feel worried as the sounds of the street faded completely, as if he had inadvertently entered another world. He couldn't hold his sigh of relief when, on the cusp of hearing, he detected the now-familiar sounds of city commerce. Following the promise of bustle, Bip eventually made his way through the winding backstreets and into a wide-open clearing.

Like all cities, Panthalus contained elements that, while not aesthetically pleasing, were essential for its day-to-day running. Sweatshops, tanners, thrift shops, and abattoirs were all needed in Panthalus, but didn't quite fit in with the specialist coffee shops and frilly tailors of the high streets. For this reason, at the rear end of the city, Grub Street had been tucked away like an embarrassing elderly relative. Bip breathed in a familiar odor as the city's bottom classes brushed and pushed past him. He heard the booming shouts of market vendors as they plied their wares—most definitely not the souvenir pots and woven place mats of the high street markets. The whole street seemed a lot more like Port Town than Panthalus, and Bip lowered a weary hand to the pommel of Brian, his trusty and as-yet-unused sword.

There seemed to be no presence of the Imperial Regulators in the swept-under sub-city of Grub Street. Perhaps because of this, the people there were louder, more boisterous, and ultimately less polite than the people of the city center. Bip flinched as, nearby, two drunken tramps began a fistfight over some unapparent difference of opinion. Bip walked away, wandering through the scrum, still slightly overawed by the hectic nature of civilization outside Kaneq, as conmen conned and hustlers hustled around him.

His attention was drawn, suddenly, by a shrill shouting that carried over the general hubbub of the street. As he made his way through the crowds, it became apparent that there was a smaller, tightly packed sub-crowd that seemed to be devoting its attention to a number of people who stood on podiums. All the people on the podiums were shouting loudly, some about politics, others about religion, some were just shouting in that random, raving way that utterly mad people shout in.

The onlookers stood with a casual interest. Some occasionally shouted back, but mostly the crowds just watched with the attitude of people with nothing else on their immediate schedules.

A large, tattered banner above the podiums read, "Speakers' Corner."

Bip pushed his way into one of the biggest audiences, where a fiery young woman with a muddy face and ruffled blond hair stood atop a podium and shouted about something with unbending zeal. The people on the neighboring podiums had given up their own personal rants to listen to the shrill, hard voice of the young speaker.

Bip tugged at the sleeve of one of the audience members. The man reluctantly looked away from the show and down at Bip.

"What do you want?" he said, natural pugnacity bending his brow.

"I was wondering if you could tell me what's going on," said Bip.

The man relaxed a bit. "That's Celia Doom," he said, pointing at the young woman on the podium. "She's off her rocker, but she puts on a bloody good show." Bip strained his ears to make out what Celia was saying.

"...and lo, with great terror, there will be a bending of the trees and a tearing of the sky, and huge balls of fire will engulf the innocent and the guilty alike. And yea, with unswerving scariness and general ill feeling, there will be rains of hard-boiled sweets that have already been sucked, and gigantic dogs will dig up the gardens of the un-wary..."

"What's she going on about?" said Bip.

"End of the world again," said the man. "Others may try it, but Celia's the best. If you want a good yarn about the coming apocalypse, then Celia's your girl."

Bip listened again, concentrating on Celia's wavering shrieks as she swung her hands through the air.

"...and people will look unto the skies and cry, 'Why? Why, oh why is this happening?' And the skies will reply, indeed, in a voice with much triteness, 'Because!' And the people will snap their fingers and say, 'Bugger!'..."

"Excuse me?"

"...and then, with great rains of treacle and terrible custard..."

"Hello?"

"...giant fish in all manner of horrible colors, verily..."

"Excuse me!"

The crowd fell into dead silence and cleared a space for Bip. Everybody watched him expectantly. Celia, frozen mid-gesture, looked down at the traveler from her podium.

"Yes?" she said.

"Well, I was just wondering," said Bip. "When is the end of the world going to happen, exactly?"

Celia rolled her eyes back in her head and lifted her hands to the sky. "Lo, when the wolf head licks at the dawn and the prices of fuel rise by a seemingly unfair amount!"

Bip blinked. "And when is that, exactly? "

"In about six weeks time...lo," said Celia.

"Oh," said Bip.

"Is there a problem with that?" Celia said testily. "Only I've got a rant to be getting on with, you know."

"Well. Sorry. But..." Bip hesitated. He had the full attention of the crowd. He had originally planned to take his warning straight to the Emperor, but, as Azron had said, it might be a good idea to build up a reputation first. Take it city by city. He took a deep breath. "Well, you see, the thing is, the end of the world probably isn't going to happen for at least another ten months. Maybe a bit less."

The crowd remained deathly silent. Celia tapped her bare foot impatiently.

"Oh, really," she said. "Well perhaps you'd like to come up here and tell us all about it yourself if you're so bloody well-informed!"

The crowd murmured its approval, and before he could protest, Bip was manhandled onto the shoddy stage. He stood before the audience. Virtually the entire crowd at Speakers' Corner was watching him now. Even the mad speakers were looking on with an amused interest.

"Not as easy as it looks, is it?" whispered Celia smugly.

"Um…" said Bip.

"Get on with it!" shouted someone.

"Yeah, either rant or sod off!" said another.

Bip took a deep breath. It was going to have to be now or never.

"Lo…" he said, then he told the story of Kaneq, the Clarions, the Volunteers, and the huge astral disaster that was heading for Bersch in roughly ten months. When he finished, the crowd stood silently, their expressions unreadable.

"Um…verily," said Bip, lamely.

The crowd remained silent until, with great deliberation, Celia stepped back onto the platform. To Bip's surprise, she turned to the crowd and held her hand in the air.

"All hail he who has been delivered by the ancient ones to foretell our coming doom! All hail the Prophet!"

The crowd roared its approval and began shaking their fists rhythmically in the air.

"*Hail! Hail! Hail!*"

"I'm sorry?" said Bip.

"*Hail!*"

"What…?"

"*Hail!*"

"I don't understand!"

Celia, who had fallen to her knees, looked up. "We are at your command, Prophet. Lead us in our hour of need!"

"Eh?"

"What would you have us do, master?"

Bip thought. "Well," he said, "I suppose you could sort of, I dunno, warn people? Warn people about the end of the world? It'd make my job a bit easier, to tell the truth."

Celia turned to the crowd once more. "You heard the wisdom of the Prophet. Go forth and spread the word! Tell the people of the coming doom! Tell them the Prophet has foretold!"

"Yeah, something like that," said Bip.

With a zealous roar, the crowd dispersed in all directions, and Bip was eventually left alone on the podium. He couldn't help feeling smug. He had, in effect, put into motion his mission to warn Bersch of the upcoming disaster. It wasn't the way he had intended to do it, but he didn't see what harm it could do to have other people spreading the word around.

He turned and began to walk down the street, feeling more optimistic than ever before. This sense of optimism stayed with him right up until a gloved hand attached to a burly arm reached out of an alleyway and dragged him inside. Bip had just enough time to recognize the gray top hat and overcoat of a Regulator before a truncheon hit him hard on the head.

As the world span rapidly and the street cobbles suddenly lay vertically rather than horizontally, Bip heard a gruff voice say, "You're under arrest, sunshine."

Then the world tuned out and all that was left was black.

2

Prisoner. Coincidence. Escape

Bip waited until the blur before him gradually turned into the face of the Imperial Regulator who had struck him, then he wished he hadn't bothered. The Regulator had the cruel features synonymous with his profession, but they extruded from an ill-shaven face framed by long ragged hair that fought bravely against the neatness of the Imperial uniform. The Regulator grinned, revealing a row of wooden teeth and a stench like some dead, forgotten thing.

"Wakey, wakey! Rise and shine!" he said.

"Oh good god, no," groaned Bip. He tried to lift a hand to the throbbing pulse on his forehead but was hindered by something heavy and clinking. He looked down at the sturdy-looking chains around his wrists and ankles. "What's going on?" he muttered.

"He wants to know what's going on." The Regulator guffawed pompously, looking around as if sharing a joke with a large group of friends. "What's going on? What's going on is that you're going down, me old matey!"

"I'm sorry, what?" said Bip.

The Regulator put on a falsetto voice and fluttered his eyelashes in what was supposedly a parody of Bip. "I'm sorry, I'm sorry!" he said. "God, your kind make me sick!"

"I have no clue what you're trying to tell me," said Bip, squinting from the pain in his head.

"You're going down, matey. Up the river! Taking the long walk!"

Bip frowned. In his muzzy state, a long walk by a river seemed quite a nice idea at the moment. "Wait a minute…" he said. "Are you trying to tell me I've been arrested?"

"Ho! College boy, eh?" said the Regulator. "You're damn tooting you've been arrested. Why do you think you're in the court house?" he said, gesturing at their surroundings.

Bip looked around. He and the Regulator were sitting in a long, poorly lit corridor, featureless bar the narrow bench they were sitting on. Down the corridor a few more unfortunates sat chained next to some other Regulators.

"Why, exactly, am I in a court house?" said Bip.

"Cuz you've been arrested, idiot!" said the Regulator.

"Yes, but, why have I been arrested?" said Bip testily.

"Oh ho!" said the Regulator, looking around, sharing the joke with his invisible friends again. "Questioning me, eh? Questioning authority? I've a good mind to give you another bump on the noggin, so I have!" He waved his gray, leather-wrapped truncheon under Bip's nose to emphasize the point.

Bip groaned as a gurgle of nausea erupted from his stomach. His head rang ceaselessly. He realized suddenly that his pack and sword were missing.

"Where are my things?" he said.

"Detained," said the Regulator. "Detained until you're found guilty. Then they'll be detained some more."

"But what If I'm found innocent?" said Bip.

"Pfft," said the Regulator and shook his head, his wide, wooden grin gleaming wetly.

Suddenly, the heavy double doors at the end of the corridor opened with a low whine. A court clerk, thin and bewigged, stood silhouetted in the doorway, peering into the dimly lit corridor.

"P.C Blungkit?" he called, squinting his eyes.

The Regulator with the wooden teeth got to his feet and dragged Bip with him. "The magistrate will see you now," said the clerk.

"Brilliant," said Blungkit, and dragged Bip down the corridor.

"Don't try to escape or I'll shoot you in the leg," he muttered as they approached the double doors, patting the pistola that rested ready on his hip. "Then I'll shoot you in the face," he added.

Bip gulped and jogged to keep up with the burly Regulator's long stride.

The courtroom, unlike the corridor leading to it, was well-decorated and spacious, lit by large windows that stretched all the way up to the high ceiling. At the far end of the room, a statue of a now-familiar figure stood blindfolded, holding a pair of scales. One of the statue's hands was lifting the blindfold slightly, allowing a stone eye to peep out from beneath.

On a large wooden pulpit, three magistrates in identical curly gray wigs and black robes sat and watched as P.C Blungkit dragged Bip before them.

"Patrol Constable Blungkit reporting, yer honors," said the Regulator.

"Oh, very good," said the central wigged man, his words heavy with disinterest. "And what is the charge?"

"Disruption of the City's Peace, Causing Public Affray and Conspiracy to Overthrow the Government, yer honor," said Blungkit.

"Now wait a bloody minute!" said Bip.

"The defendant will wait until addressed before speaking," snapped the judge. He gestured to Blungkit, who promptly clipped Bip around the ear.

"Ow," said Bip.

"Quiet, you," Blungkit whispered, before flicking Bip's nose. Bip blinked rapidly but wisely held back any verbal retort.

"Now, where were we?" said the judge. "Ah yes, conspiracy to overthrow the government? These are serious charges, Blungkit. Have you any proof?"

"Well, yer honor, I caught him on Speakers' Corner saying how the end of the world was coming and how something needed to be done about it. Sounded a bit political, if you get my meaning."

The judge peered at some paperwork before him, mainly doodles and scribbles that had accumulated over a long, uneventful day.

"Rather flimsy grounds for conspiracy to terrorism, isn't it? 'Sounded a bit political'?"

"Ah, but people were listening to him!" said Blungkit.

The magistrate raised a bushy eyebrow. "Listening? To the speakers? Whatever next?" He stifled a yawn before continuing. "As much as I admire your enthusiasm, Blungkit, I have to say this is an encroachment on my lunch hour. Now, unless this man has actually done any real harm to the city, you can just throw him in the holding tanks with the rest of the scum."

"Hey!" Bip cried indignantly, and was promptly clipped around the ear again.

"Shut it, you!" said Blungkit, then hastily added, "Not you, yer honor.'

One of the magistrates, who had been napping, awoke suddenly and looked about, smacking his lips. "Isn't it lunchtime?" he muttered.

"Your observance is duly noted. Let the record show that it is indeed nearly lunchtime," said the central magistrate. "Now, Blungkit, let's wrap this up quickly, shall we? What exactly did the defendant say to disrupt the peace?"

As Blungkit began to recount his tale, Bip's attention wandered gloomily to the view of freedom just outside the courthouse windows. He was beginning to wonder if his luck could get much worse when, as if on cue, the light in the courthouse seemed to dim, and Blungkit's booming rhetoric seemed to slow and reverberate weirdly. A general feeling of wrongness that felt somehow familiar began to sink into Bip's brain. He looked around to see if anyone else had noticed the sudden change in the environment, and that was when, to his shock, he saw Mr. Random sitting casually on the magistrate's pulpit, his bald, red head and pointy ears gleaming in the afternoon light. The demonic figure smiled his razor grin and wiggled his spindly fingers in greeting.

Mouthing like a guppy, Bip looked about the room to see if anyone else had noticed the intruder. Mr. Random's smile widened as he wagged his finger at Bip, reminding the Kaneqian that no one else would be able to see him.

As Blungkit's now oddly slow voice continued to drawl, Mr. Random leaned over to the ear of the bored-looking magistrate and began whispering, smiling his metal smile all the while, as the magistrate's expression of vague amusement gradually hardened into a look of serious concentration, until he was glaring fiercely at Bip.

Mr. Random stepped back and tipped Bip a wink before clicking his fingers and disappearing with a pop. Reality snapped back to normal as if it had been stretched out like a rubber band.

"...so then I hit him in the face with my truncheon and here we are!" Blungkit finished chirpily.

The courtroom was utterly silent. The magistrates, who had formerly been so blasé, were now all sitting rigid, focusing identically furious stares at Bip. The central magistrate rose to his feet.

"I suppose you think that poisoning the minds of our people with your hysterical stories is acceptable behavior?" he said, his words withering with spite.

"...no?" said Bip.

"I suppose you think it's rather amusing to spread unnecessary fear and doubt in an otherwise content community?"

"...no?" said Bip.

Suddenly, the magistrate slammed his fist into the pulpit. "I will not have raving troublemakers mocking our city folk!" he roared.

"Woah!" said Bip. "Steady on!"

"Shut it, you," Blungkit growled.

The magistrate, shaking with fury, leveled a crooked finger at Bip. "So you're a doomsayer, eh?" he said. "It seems to me that a chap spouting on about the end of the world can't be considered normal behavior in a civilized society." The magistrate began to grin, revealing neat little teeth, clenched tightly. "I say we put him with the other loons and troublemakers!" The magistrate waved a small, ornate gavel and pounded it sharply on the pulpit. "Six months!" he screeched. "Six months in the Bin!"

The other magistrates leapt to their feet and began applauding manically as Bip was dragged away by Blungkit.

"You're for it now, mate," said the Regulator. "I knew you were trouble, but I didn't think they'd stick you in the Bin."

"What's the Bin?"

"It's where they stick the incurably insane! No one who goes in ever comes out!"

"But I'm not crazy!"

"If you're not crazy now, you will be soon," laughed Blungkit.

"No, please!" Bip wailed, turning around to plead with the impassive magistrates.

"I'm not crazy! I'm not lying! If you don't let me go you're all doomed! Doomed! Do you hear?!"

Blungkit unsheathed his truncheon and rapped Bip smartly on the head, knocking him out cold for the second time that day.

"That's exactly what I'd expect a crazy person to say," he muttered, and dragged the Kaneqian's limp form to the Bin.

THE BIN, formerly known as St. Dott's Hospital for the Less Than Sane, was situated on the outskirts of Panthalus, standing dark and alone like a trench-coated pervert in a park. What had once been a magnificent building typical of the Panthalus style of architecture had decayed and rotted into a black and rusted aberration, slimy with moss and riddled with disrepair, as if the very insanity that inhabited the hospital had twisted the structure like a monstrous cancer.

The Bin was ancient, one of the oldest buildings in Panthalus, and was so crushed and uneven in some places that it seemed to erupt organically from the ground rather than having been built on top of it. Its crumbling tower pierced the setting sun, shading the building to pitch as the cries of the mad drifted eerily on the twilight breeze.

Inside, tucked into one of the blackest and most crumbled wings of the hospital-cum-prison, Bip lay slumped on a bare slab floor. He shivered, coming around to the feel of cold stone on his cheek. His vision cleared to reveal the waxing moon rising through the bars of a narrow window.

"Oh, crap," he said, remembering the courtroom.

He sat up and immediately regretted doing so as pain swam through his head like a sea turtle. Yeah. A sea turtle with spikes. A great big angry spiky sea turtle. Bip wondered briefly if he had been knocked unconscious too many times in one day and dismissed the unusual analogy with a shake of his head.

He looked around. His cell wasn't going to win any awards for originality. Three stone walls, another wall consisting of iron bars and a heavy-looking door.

Damp? Check. Cobwebs? Check. Rats? Check.

He froze as a lunatic howl rang out from some dark and lonely corner. He shivered again and turned his attention to the corridor on the other side of the cell's bars. Beyond was Blungkit, kicked back on a chair by a desk a comfortable distance away from the cell, a single candle illuminating his ragged face. Apparently, he had been on guard duty and had fallen asleep. He was snoring with unexpected gentleness, his gray top hat lowered over his eyes. Bip could just make out the bulk of his rucksack and Brian lying at the Regulator's feet. He sighed. There was no chance of reaching either of them.

"I expect he's going to steal them."

Bip whipped around to face the darkness behind him. In a corner blotted thickly with shadow, a man of unidentifiable age emerged, his face hidden by long straggling hair and a beard of monolithic proportions. His features were incredibly pale and drawn, almost translucent in the silvery moonlight, and he was thick with dust.

"They're supposed to register your belongings and store them. They don't, though. More often than not, they just steal them," said the man, his voice cracked and quiet as if he hadn't spoken for a long time.

Bip took a step back from the cell-dweller, unconsciously moving his hand down to a sword hilt that was no longer there. "Who are you?" he demanded.

The man ignored the question. "You look familiar..." he said. "Have I known you, friend?"

"I shouldn't think so," said Bip. "I don't really hang around with crazy people..." His thoughts turned treacherously to Glimton and Rynford. "Much," he added.

"I know your face, I'm sure," said the man, peering at Bip. "You look a lot like...a friend of mine. But you couldn't be. Couldn't be." The man slumped back against the damp, glistening walls.

Bip, realizing that perhaps the stranger wasn't a threat after all, sat down against the bars of the cell. "How long have you been in here?" he asked.

The cell-dweller waved his hand at the wall above his head. Bip peered through the darkness and gasped as he noticed the incredible number of tiny notches scraped painstakingly into the stonework. It would take a long while to count them all properly, he guessed—probably a full day or so.

"Do they represent days, those notches?" said Bip, gaping.

"No," said the prisoner. "Months."

Bip looked at the thousands of notches. "Impossible!" he scoffed. "That'd make you at least..." Bip tried to estimate the sum total of the notches and gave up.

The man looked up and fixed Bip with a weary stare. "At least," he said.

Bip decided not to labor the point, thinking it best not to argue with anyone residing in a hospital/prison for the incurably insane. He whistled and clucked for a while, tapping his hands on his knees.

"So," he said, eventually. "What did they lock you up for, then?"

The man frowned in concentration. "Long time ago," he said. "Hard to remember. I had a message. A warning. Very important. Don't know what happened. Been here ever since."

"Oh," said Bip. "A doomsayer. That's what the judge called it. I don't know what it means, though. I had a warning as well, about the end of the world. No one seemed to care too much, though—they just threw me in here."

"You lose your memory after a while," said the man suddenly. "It gets harder to remember how things were. Harder to remember the earlier years. Being cooped up in here doesn't help much either."

Bip wondered how he should reply and then, not able to think of anything polite to say, decided to change the subject. "Have you been by yourself all this time?" he said.

"Oh, no," said the man. "I have this rubber ball to play with. Without it, I probably would have gone nuts a long time ago." The man pulled a withered rubber ball from the recesses of his ragged clothing. On the ball a small smiley face had been drawn in black ink. "I call him Bertie," said the man. "He doesn't talk much, but he's a great listener."

Bip smiled politely and thought of something nice to say. "…good?" he managed.

"Yeah. Me and Bertie have some laughs," said the prisoner. As if to demonstrate, he threw Bertie lightly toward a wall. The ball impacted and fell to the ground with a slump, barely rolling let alone bouncing. "Happy times," said the man.

Bip smiled politely and thought desperately of escape. If he could just reach his pack, he thought, he could surely get out of here. He knew that one of Glimton's reprogrammed acorns had FILE inscribed upon it, and he was pretty sure he had seen one called CUNNING DISGUISE. He needed to think fast before Blungkit awoke and, as was more than likely, made off with his possessions.

"What did you say your name was?" said the prisoner, distracting Bip from his scheming.

"I'm Bip," said Bip. "What's your name?"

The man ignored him again. "What were you saying about the end of the world?" he said, after a while.

"What?" said Bip, testily, annoyed by being distracted from the problem of escape.

"You mentioned the end of the world. Said you had a warning?"

"Oh, yes." Bip reasoned that it couldn't do any harm to tell a crazy person that the planet was going to explode soon. Thinking about it, crazy people probably said the same type of thing all the time. "I was sent from a place called Kaneq to warn the world of an astral disaster." Bip turned back to fiddling with the solid lock on the cell door.

Suddenly he felt a hand around his neck and was lifted roughly into the air. He looked down into the wild eyes of the cell-dweller, all of a sudden seeming far from harmless.

"What did you say?" the prisoner hissed through clenched teeth.

"Disaster?" squeaked Bip.

"Before that! "

"Astral?"

"Before that!" screamed the prisoner, shaking Bip by the scruff of his jumper.

"Kaneq?" wailed Bip.

The prisoner dropped Bip immediately and began pacing the small cell, muttering continuously under his breath. "Kanick. Kaneq. It can't be! It can't be!" he said.

"Can't be what?" said Bip, rubbing his sore neck.

The prisoner whirled around and pointed an accusing finger at Bip. "Quiet, you!" he shouted. "You're not real!"

Bip didn't know what to say. It was the first time anyone had accused him of not existing.

"You can't be real. Some sick joke. I've gone mad! This time I've really gone mad!" wailed the stranger.

Bip wondered what to say. Now that he was at his full height, the prisoner looked quite formidable compared to when he had been huddled by the wall.

"I am real!" said Bip, then added, "Sorry."

The prisoner froze in his pacing and approached Bip. Then, without warning, he poked him hard in the eye.

"Arrgh!" screamed Bip. "For the love of god, man, what did you do that for?!" he wailed.

"Unbelievable," said the prisoner. "Impossible...of all the chances."

"My eye! My eye!" cried Bip.

"You're really from Kanick?" said the man.

"Kaneq! Yes, you mad bastard! That really hurt, you know!"

The prisoner got down on one knee, bringing his head level with Bip's. "The people who first came to Kanick...Kaneq. Who were they? Do you know?"

"The Clarions," said Bip, frowning. "Why?'

"And what was their purpose there?" said the man urgently.

"They were supposed to be watching over things, but they crashed and... Look, what are you getting at?"

The prisoner rose to his feet and offered a hand to Bip, who accepted and stood up, still rubbing his eye. "I think you and I may have something in common," said the prisoner. "My name is Handen Strike. I came from Kaneq to save the world."

THERE WERE EXPLANATIONS. Plenty of explanations. About the Clarions and the volunteers, the Discordance and the Sentinel. About what had happened to Bip. About what had happened to Handen.

There were gaps in Handen's story. He remembered about the fountain of youth, his time in Kaneq, and his life on the home world of Clarion, all memories that seemed like half-forgotten dreams now. But there was much he couldn't remember, a little over a millennium of memories being too much for one brain to handle. He could not, for instance, remember how he had come to be imprisoned. He only knew that he had been locked away for centuries, eventually forgotten about and dismissed as a madman, slowly beginning to believe that he was a madman.

"You don't know how happy this makes me!" said Handen, half crying and half laughing with ambivalent emotion that would have seemed quite melodramatic to the man he had been so many centuries ago. "I was beginning to think that I was insane! That Kanick and the rest of it was just the demented dream of a madman!"

"Well. It wasn't," said Bip, matter-of-factly.

"You try being locked up for a couple of centuries with no one to convince you of what's real and what's not but a rubber ball named Bertie—then we'll see how confident you are in your memories," Handen chided.

"A fair point," said Bip. "But I'm still having trouble taking all this in. You're the first volunteer?" Bip gestured to the emaciated, scraggly figure before him.

"I haven't exactly been getting much exercise lately," said Handen reproachfully. "Well this is good news! Great news!" said Bip eventually. "I'm sure with the two of us corroborating our story, they'll be bound to believe us!"

Handen raised an eyebrow. "I remind you that we're in a prison for the insane. No one's going to believe anything we say. I've tried a million times to explain. Literally a million."

"Oh," said Bip. "So we're stuck, then?"

"A few hundred years ago, I would've had no trouble wrestling past the guards and getting the girl before being chased down a corridor by a fiery explosion," Handen muttered mournfully.

"What?" said Bip.

"Oh, nothing," said Handen, shaking his head. "Trust me, kid, I've thought of everything to escape from here, but the security's too great. They put you under full restraint any time they're going to open the cell, and they rarely open the cell anyway. No one leaves any convenient cutlery, and I sure as hell haven't had any hacksaws baked into cakes delivered."

"Oh." Bip couldn't help feeling downcast.

"Cheer up," said Handen. "At least you'll probably die in here in a couple of months. I don't even have that luxury."

"Hey!" said Bip.

"Sorry," said Handen sheepishly. "You get used to just saying what's on your mind when you've had no one to talk to but a ball for years."

Bip, unimpressed with the idea of wasting away in a cell, thought manically of an escape plan. "If I could just get my pack, I could get us out of here, I know it," he said.

They looked over at the slouching form of Blungkit. He had

managed to sleep soundly through Handen and Bip's entire encounter.

"We could make a rope from our clothes?" said Bip.

"Wouldn't work," said Handen. "There'd be nothing to snag the pack with, and it's too large to lasso."

The two prisoners looked at the pack, both thinking hard. "Say!" said Handen. "Any chance you're Elite-Gifted?"

"I'm a what now?" said Bip.

"Elite-Gifted? Gifted? Journeyman?"

"I'm sorry, I'm not following you," said Bip.

"Have you honed your innate talent to manipulate the building blocks of existence with the power of your mind?" said Handen testily.

"Oh, you mean am I a psyentist?" said Bip.

"Sure. Whatever. Are you?"

"Not a very good one," confessed Bip. "What about you? You're Kaneqian, can't you do any psyence?"

"I was a Hostilities Advisor—I never had the training to hone my abilities."

"You were a what?"

"A Hostilities Advisor? A Security Liaison? A Defence Marshall?"

"You mean like a Hunter?" said Bip.

"Yeah, I guess," said Handen. "If you want anybody to beat someone up, then I'm your man, but I can't really help you with the door problem."

"Oh," said Bip.

"Yeah," said Handen.

The two looked at the pack some more as the gentle whistle of Blungkit's snoring filled the corridor outside the cell.

"Are you sure you couldn't, you know, persuade the rucksack to move over here?" said Handen after a while.

Bip thought hard. Trying to move the pack itself would be risky, but it occurred to him that he could try something similar to the podium trick he had attempted at the apprentice fair. If he could slope the stone floor upward underneath the pack, then gravity would roll the pack toward him. He would just have to hope he didn't set his feet on fire again.

"Stand back," said Bip. Handen obliged as Bip closed his eyes and concentrated, focusing his mind on the stone floor, sensing the common energies that entwined all matter, living and inanimate.

Bip concentrated...

Concentrated...

With a mighty whoosh, Blungkit's chair suddenly expanded into a huge white dome, crushing the sleeping Regulator against the ceiling and exploding the desk into shards of wood. Bip ducked as the brass candlestick sailed over his head.

After the creaking noises stopped, Bip looked out from behind his fingers, noticing his breath steaming in the sudden iciness of the room. A huge white igloo stood where the sleeping Regulator had once been.

Damn, thought Bip. *If it's not random incinerations, it's bloody igloos.* Handen slowly stood up from the corner he had instinctively dived into.

"Impressive," he said. "Unorthodox, but impressive."

Bip followed the man's gaze and realized that the sudden appearance of the igloo had shoved both Brian and his pack toward the cell. The sword was just out of reach, but the rucksack was in easy grabbing distance. Bip stretched his arms through the bars of the cell and retrieved his pack. He then began rummaging through the contents.

"What've you got in there?" said Handen. "A saw? A lockpick?"

"Even better!" Bip waggled a bag of acorns under Handen's nose.

"Oh," said Handen, nonplussed. "A bag of nuts. Now we're talking. What're you going to do, flick them at the guards and hope they'll surrender?'

"Of course not," said Bip, looking carefully at each acorn in turn. "These are reprogrammed acorns. You just add water, and they turn into something useful."

"Really," said Handen. "And you're absolutely sure they didn't throw you in here because you're crazy?"

"Aha!" cried Bip triumphantly. He had come across an acorn that had the word KEY inscribed on it. Bip put the acorn in his mouth and swished it around a few times. He then held the nut, glistening with spit, close to the keyhole on the cell door.

Handen watched with growing amazement as the nut began to sprout little green tendrils that waved around until they eventually slithered into the keyhole. There was a pause as a few more shoots grew, then an audible click as the lock opened. The heavy cell door swung inward with a gentle groan.

"Very impressive," said Handen.

"Yeah, they're pretty handy," said Bip. "Now what do we do?"

Handen smirked. There was a glint in his eye that hadn't been there for centuries. He stepped out into the corridor and threw Brian to Bip, who caught the sword awkwardly by the scabbard. Then Handen went over to the unconscious form of Blungkit and retrieved a heavy wooden truncheon and the flintlock pistola. Handen weighed the two weapons carefully in his hand and checked the sights of the pistola.

"Not quite a las-blaster," he muttered, "but it'll do…"

Handen tied his long beard in a knot and held his long hair back in a ponytail tied with a scrap of his clothing.

"What are you going to do?" said Bip.

Handen grinned a dangerous grin. "I'm going to walk right out of here. And nobody is going to stop me."

BIP AND HANDEN walked through the front gate of the Bin. The night guard waved them through dismissively. Handen tipped his top hat in greeting and adjusted the collar of his long, gray coat.

"You know," Bip whispered, "when you said you weren't going to be stopped, I sort of envisioned you fighting your way out against insurmountable odds, for some reason."

"Yeah, well, insurmountable odds are for when you have the time to deal with them," said Handen, clinking Blungkit's purse in his hands. "Right now, what I want is a warm bed, something good to eat, and maybe a drink or two. Or six."

The two Kaneqians walked back toward Panthalus as the moon hung lazily in the sky.

A few hours later, Blungkit awoke to find himself naked and shivering in a rapidly melting Igloo.

3

Curse of the Hero

The Ugly Swan was one of the nicer taverns in Grub Street, far enough from the hurly-burly to attract a more sedate clientele, but close enough to provide the comforting anonymity of regular and varied custom.

Inside, a large log fire warmed the pub against the night's chill, popping expletively as it sent sparks like tiny demons rushing through the cobbled chimney. Groups of drinkers huddled around large oak tables, washed in languid candlelight, their shadows flickering softly against the heavy oak beams of the ceiling. The sound of trivial conversation was muffled and softened by the thick animal skins that hung from roof to floor, absorbing the heat from the fire and warming the room cozily.

Handen and Bip sat at the bar, each with a large mug of bitter ale before him, while Handen regaled Bip with a few of the adventures (he spat the word) he had faced on his quest to reach the Empire's capital. The barman washed a glass in polite silence while a young waitress, a scrawny, pretty thing, struggled with an armload of empty glasses and took every opportunity to smile coyly at Handen. Handen returned the smiles, relishing the sight of a woman after centuries of solitude.

The former prisoner had taken the time to neaten himself up, and in doing so had changed his appearance significantly. He had spent Blungkit's money and some of Bip's gold on some new clothes and equipment, including a sturdy leather coat and riding boots, which he wore over a comfortable shirt and trousers. His second port of call had been a blacksmith's and supply store, where he had purchased, amongst other things, a weighty bastard sword and a well-oiled leather whip, as well as various daggers and throwing knives, which he had strapped and secreted about his person. His mood had brightened considerably once he had a few sharp objects to hand.

Bip had been quite surprised to see his new companion emerge, finally, from the barber's. His scraggly beard had been shaved away to reveal the perpendicular lines of a heavy, heroic jaw, and his wild-man hair was now combed back into a smooth and rigid side parting. Far from the ageless, hollow appearance of the mad prisoner Bip had first met, Handen had revealed himself to be a handsome man in his mid-thirties, with dark, severe features that seemed to complement the still-haunted look in his eyes. And now he sat, clean of face and neat of collar, his satchel and scabbard by his side and the Regulator's pilfered pistola holstered over his hip. Only a few hours ago Handen had resembled nothing but the pathetic madman his years of imprisonment had made him. Now he looked every ounce the adventurer he had once been.

The improvements in Handen's appearance had also turned out to be an ideal disguise, considering that the Regulators were doubtless pursuing them by now. With this in mind, Bip had also attempted to disguise himself using the CUNNING DISGUISE acorn in his pack, but had discovered that a false moustache and glasses made entirely of bracken were more conspicuous than he would have liked, especially seeing as he already wore glasses anyway. So he opted to sit in the corner and just concentrate on being inconspicuous instead.

"...so then I rescued the girl, blew up the embassy, and escaped on a raft before the volcano erupted," said Handen, finishing his story and taking a long pull from his pint mug.

"Fascinating," said Bip, who, frankly, thought Handen was exaggerating somewhat. He took a close look at his fellow Kaneqian. He was looking a lot healthier than when they had left the Bin—not just the haircut, shave, and clean clothes, but even his complexion seemed to have improved. He even seemed to have put on weight.

"You're looking well," said Bip, suspiciously.

"One of the benefits of immortality," said Handen. "I heal quickly. Very quickly." Bip raised a doubtful eyebrow.

Handen sighed. "You don't believe me, do you?" he said.

"It's a bit far-fetched," conceded Bip.

Without warning, Handen crushed the thick glass pint mug in his hand with a sudden and sparkling crash. Both the barman and Bip jumped in shock as a thin wave of blood erupted soundlessly from the adventurer's palm.

"Sorry about that," said Handen, chirpily. "Must have been a faulty glass."

The barman nodded, puzzled concern etched over his face. "Do you want a bandage for your hand?" he said.

Handen waved his gory palm in front of Bip's face. It was covered in blood.

"No thanks," he said pointedly. "It's not as bad as it looks." With that, he wiped his hand clean with a bar towel, then waved it in front of Bip's face again. "See?" he said. There was not a trace of damage to the hand. Not even a scratch.

"Point taken," said Bip, weakly.

Handen ordered another mug of ale and drank with gusto. "By God, that's good," he said. "Five hundred years or more without a pint certainly builds up a thirst."

Bip was still gazing, dumbfounded, at Handen's hand. "Didn't that hurt?" he asked.

"What?" said Handen, distractedly. "Oh that. Yeah, it hurts, but only for a minute."

"So you really are immortal then? Completely invulnerable?"

"Apparently," said Handen. "I've been shot, stabbed, hanged, disembowelled, decapitated, and defenestrated." He took another mouthful of the bitter ale. "Though I've yet to experiment with being eaten or burnt alive. I can't imagine they'd be much fun."

"Must be nice," Bip concluded.

Handen paused with his mug to his lips. He turned a narrow eye on Bip. "Have you any idea how boring life gets after a couple of centuries of existence?" he said.

"…no?" said Bip.

"Of course you haven't," said Handen. "Let me tell you, when you've done all there is to do, life gets very dull very fast, and knowing you can't die takes all the fun out of it, too. And you know the worst part? I didn't even get to spend a near millennium of immortality relaxing and seeing the sights! When I wasn't being plagued by countless intrepid adventures, I was locked up in that damned cell!" The immortal drained the remainder of his pint mug, banged the glass on the bar, and signaled for a refill.

Bip looked at his new friend with open curiosity. "How many of these intrepid adventures have you had, then?" he said.

"I dunno," said Handen glumly. "Thousands. I lost count a long time ago. There's only so many evil masterminds you can foil and lost tombs you can raid before they all start to look alike."

"Really?" said Bip.

"A man once called it The Curse of the Hero," said Handen, peering back into ancient memories. "At the time I thought he was just winding me up, but the more I think about it, the more I realize he might have had a point. You see, the average guy, if he's lucky—or unlucky, I should say—chances are he'll get one great adventure in his lifetime. Me? I get about three or four a year."

"I'm sorry," said Bip, shaking his head. "It's a bit much to take in."

Handen sighed and then glanced around the room for a while. "There is a way to test the theory," he concluded, eventually. "You see that man over there?" He pointed to a group of drunken regulars; a few of them were significantly burlier than their friends. The largest, a multi-scarred brute with a glass eye, was glaring directly at Handen. "He's the top dog around here, and I'm guessing he's not too fond of strangers coming into his local and attracting the attention of the waitress he fancies." Handen pointed to the waitress, who blushed and looked away.

"What's your point?" said Bip, unsure of where the conversation was going and a little jealous of the waitress's obvious interest in Handen, who, only a few hours ago, had been a stinking, fish-pale madman in a cell.

"Well," said Handen. "What usually happens in this situation is, the big guy comes up and picks a fight with me, punches are thrown, suddenly the whole bar erupts into a brawl, someone swings from the chandelier—or any other appropriate lighting fixture—and a couple of people are thrown through windows. Then I get the girl and escape in the commotion. Sometimes there is someone playing a piano, but not always."

"You can't be sure of that," scoffed Bip.

"Just watch, kid. There's nothing I can do about it," replied Handen.

At the back of the bar, the pianist began to play an upbeat honky-tonk rhythm.

He didn't really know why—he usually specialized in slow, bluesy folk—but something deep in his bones told him that honky-tonk music was required.

Handen raised a smug eyebrow at Bip as he felt a hand tap him on the shoulder. He turned around to face the barrel chest of the brute that had been staring at him, then craned his neck to look the challenger—who towered over him by a good foot and a half—in the eye. The regular, doubtless the champion of the Ugly Swan and the type of person for whom violence solves everything, glared down with open hostility, a thin sliver of beer-stinking dribble hanging from his oversized chops as he prepared to speak.

Handen interjected before the man could say anything. "What's it to be, then?" he asked chirpily. "The 'We don't like your sort around here' or the 'What are you looking at?'"

The brute looked confused for a moment. He had the unsettling sensation that someone had changed the script just as he'd walked on stage.

"I tell you what," said Handen. "Why don't we spare some time and get right to the point?" Then he rocketed his fist as hard as he could into the brute's mouth.

PUNCHES WERE THROWN. A brawl erupted. Somebody swung from the chandelier and somebody else was thrown through a window. Someone was even comically thrown across the length of the bar. The piano player played on regardless, aware, on some deep spiritual level, that he had a duty to perform.

LATER ON, Bip and Handen sat against a wall in an alleyway, Handen tending bruises that were already beginning to heal while, by his side, the awestruck waitress gaped at him with open hero-worship.

"Point taken," said Bip, breathing heavily. He had ducked under a table for the majority of the brawl and had consequently avoided injury. He was quite shaken, though.

"I told you," said Handen

"That was pretty exciting stuff," said Bip, checking his pulse.

"Really? I thought I was a bit rusty, to tell you the truth," said Handen. "It's been a while, I'll admit, but it's like riding a bike, really— it all comes back to you."

"Yeah, but when you jumped over that guy's head and kicked him in the bum!" said Bip excitedly.

"Nothing special," said Handen.

"But what about when you ran up the wall and back-flipped onto the bar?" said Bip.

"Pretty standard stuff, really."

"And when you upper-cutted that chap and he fell through the table?"

"That? Oh, that's basic bar brawl fare, that."

"Well I thought it was pretty exciting," huffed Bip.

"You get used to it," said Handen glumly. He looked down at the waitress on his arm. She couldn't have been older than sixteen. "Look, miss," he said. "You probably think I'm going to drag you off on some romantic and dashing adventure..."

The waitress nodded enthusiastically.

"Well ordinarily I would, but I'm sort of in the middle of something at the minute so I can't, really."

The waitress looked crestfallen.

"Sorry," said Handen, "but it's for your own good. I'm sure you're busy enough with your own life without having some dangerously bold escapade to spoil your week."

The young girl tilted her head in thought. "Well I do have to cook the breakfasts tomorrow...and then there's the barrel deliveries..." she said reluctantly.

"Off you go, then—don't worry about us."

The waitress scuttled back to the Ugly Swan, occasionally glancing hopefully back over her shoulder. Handen watched her leave.

"Sorry about that," he said, turning to Bip. "I don't know why I brought her with us. Force of habit I suppose."

"I see," said Bip. "So what happens now?"

Handen thought for a minute. After so many years locked away from society, there were plenty of things he wanted to do, but time was running out.

"So we have roughly ten months until the end of the world?" he said.

"Yep," said Bip.

"So much time wasted," said Handen, looking up at the stars. "I wonder why no one has come?"

The two stared up at the clear midnight skies for a while. The stars blinked and danced impassively. No answer came.

"We have to reach the capital," said Bip.

"Are you sure that's such a good idea?" said Handen. "You've seen what happens when you try to tell people about the end of the world. How can we be sure it won't happen again?"

"We can't," said Bip. "But I don't have any better ideas, do you? "

Handen thought for a while. "No," he concluded.

"Then we go to the capital."

Handen rose to his feet. "You realize that the law will be after us now? That our faces will be known to every soldier and Regulator across the Empire? That we'll have to cross miles of hostile territory, sleeping and eating only where we can, hiding and living in fear?"

"Actually, I didn't think of that," said Bip. "Oh dear."

"Don't worry about it," said Handen grimly. "I used to do this sort of thing all the time."

THE FIRST THING Handen had done to prepare for their flight was to purchase a map, having lost his along with the rest of his equipment several hundred years ago. Bip and Handen now sat in the back room of a nondescript inn, poring over the paper geography before them, which showed the entire continent of Regalious, including Panthalus and Argustin, the capital city. The continent was at least four times the size of the Free Countries, and their destination looked dismayingly far away.

The travelers agreed that the journey would have to be made by cart and foot, avoiding any public transport, as the security measures in the airports and crawlertrams were too risky for wanted felons. However, even the journey by foot was not free of the risk of capture. To travel comfortably the shortest distance between Panthalus and Argustin, they would have to pass through many cities, hamlets, and other well-fortified locations that were bound to hold an inconvenient number of law enforcers.

At first, Bip thought Handen was perhaps being a bit paranoid about the level of interest the Regulators would show for two escaped mental patients. Handen had answered Bip's doubts by taking a short walk around the city and coming back with an armload of wanted posters, all bearing Bip and Handen's description and some rough artists "impressions." Apparently assaulting a Regulator was a hanging offence, and Blungkit had obviously pressed that this was the case.

Eventually the two fugitives decided that they would have to extend their trip to avoid capture, venturing south into the less-marshaled provinces of Regalious, crossing the Bone Desert, then east through the Dozantyne Shrub before swinging back north into the Empire's heart. The eventual route of the journey looked especially difficult on paper and promised to be more so in practice, adding months onto their estimated traveling time and increasing their potential provision budget by as much as ten times.

"We'll have to live off the land," Handen had said. "There's no way short of banditry we can finance the whole trip by ourselves."

"But what about my gold?" said Bip.

Handen shook his head. "There's a lot to consider. The purchase of a well-built wagon, food and supplies, fresh horses and, of course, when we reach the capital, we'll probably need bribe money. If we can provide our own food, we can cut our costs significantly."

To this end, Handen purchased a longbow and a few long spears. It was agreed that even with Bip's limited experience, the two of them would be able to hunt enough quarry to keep themselves in adequate supply of meat, hopefully with enough left over to trade for vegetables and cereals. Of course, the downside to fending and foraging for themselves as they went along was that they would have to further delay their estimated time of arrival at Argustin. Currently, Handen was guessing that the complete journey would take three to four months, depending on the weather and their luck.

After a short rest, Handen and Bip took to the city in the early hours of the morning. They searched Grub Street high and low for a wagon that was for sale and in an adequate state of repair, but with little luck. Eventually, they convinced a traveling merchant to part with his wagon and two horses for a price that was less than fair. Handen had thought about haggling but had quickly decided that it was worth the price to be out of Panthalus as soon as possible. They had even convinced the merchant, for an extra fee, to ride them out of the city while they hid in the covered section of the wagon, to avoid attracting the attention of the gatekeepers.

And so, a safe distance from Panthalus, the two Kaneqians began their expedition to Argustin, heading across the rolling farmlands toward an uncertain destiny.

THEY MOVED BY NIGHT, wrapping themselves in thick shadows to stay hidden, whispering breathy conversations only when the silence became too much to bear. They stole across landscapes stained silver by a treacherous moon, ducking behind hills, and weaving between trees as they inched slowly toward what they hoped would be sanctuary.

Their days were harsh and repetitive, their rigid schedule ensuring they covered as much ground as possible. When they rested in the anxious pre-dawn, crammed hidden between hedges or heather, Handen would cover the wagon in bracken and leaves, camouflaging it from casual observation and providing some insulation against the early morning mists. They would sleep, listening to the rain pattering on the wagon's canvas like a gentle intruder, and awake in the afternoons, eating what they had saved or foraged before moving on again.

Occasionally, at sporadic intervals, Handen would cross over rivers or travel up streams, doubling back and forth, cutting complex trails in the furze to confuse anyone who might be tracking them. For the days and weeks they traveled in the Panthalus province, Bip reflected, it seemed as though they were holding their breath at every waking moment, listening for the sure signs that the unseen enemy was creeping at their backs.

And they were right to do so. Spreading like a virus, like bad news and rumors, the description of two "dangerous escaped criminals" was circulating around the police quarters and guardhouses, the tight pockets of bounty hunters and the squalid drinking dens of mercenaries. A large, terrible, and invisible fist was closing slowly around the two fugitives, and though they didn't know it for sure, they could feel the pressure of it in their chests every night, as a twig snapped close by or a bush rustled in the dark.

They knew the abject terror of the ultimate paranoid. The world was out to get them.

Not much was shared between the two fugitives as they traveled, bar the occasional casual dialogue to remind themselves that they were still human and not the drifting ghosts they had come to feel like. Occasionally, though, the two would encounter moments of comfort and security, abandoned barns or unoccupied huts, where they could talk and learn more about each other.

Bip would tell Handen about Kaneq, the adventurer astonished by how such a small settlement had survived for so long in isolation, and proud about the still-integral existence of the hunting party he had founded so many centuries before. In turn, Bip would sit astounded at Handen's tales of other worlds and peoples and of his adventures on Bersch before their chance encounter.

Their conversations provided not just companionship, but a useful pooling of knowledge. Though Handen's experience of the topography of Regalious was vastly outdated, it still served as a rough guide to their journey, allowing them to travel with a degree of certainty rather than blindly following the markings on their maps. Bip, for his part, was able to apply his limited experience of modern civilization on Bersch.

One opportunity for more relaxed conversation saw the travelers camped in the shell of a burnt-out farmhouse, its blackened beams testament to some tragedy long since past. Bip and Handen sat in the relative shelter of what was once a kitchen, clustered around some likely-looking rubble that might support a fire. At one end of the room, their two horses stood wrapped in blankets and rummaging in nosebags. One of the horses, though recently rubbed down, was sweating hard and breathing heavily.

"I think Wynona's sick," said Bip.

Handen looked puzzled. "Who's Wynona? "

"The horse. The one with the patch on its side."

Handen looked over. "I think you're right. We'll ride them for another full day and then take it easy until we can find a place to trade."

"But what if she's too sick to ride?"

Handen looked at his friend. Though they had been on the road for some time now, Bip still seemed naïve about some of the harsher realities of being on the run. "If she's too sick to ride, we take her downwind, butcher her, and then pack the meat for stock and trade. Then we carry on."

Bip's eyes widened. "Butcher Wynona? We can't do that!"

Handen sighed. "We may have to. We don't have the time or resources to look after her, you know that." Bip looked crestfallen. "Look," Handen continued. "In the long run, if she gets too sick, it'll be more of a kindness to kill her quickly rather than leave her to die."

Bip thought for a moment. "Will it? So you'd rather be chopped up into pieces and eaten than be left to die peacefully?"

"Yes."

"Don't lie!"

"Okay then, no. But the point is, we can't afford to waste resources, and like it or not, that's what 'Wynona' is: a resource!" said Handen.

Bip went quiet for a minute, staring at the floor. "Well, what about Gertrude?"

"Who's Gertrude?"

"The other horse!"

"Well, what about her?"

"She can't pull the cart by herself! She'll get knackered!"

Handen put a hand over his eyes, more tired, all of a sudden, than he had been in centuries. "We can get other horses," he said.

"Doesn't seem right," huffed Bip. "Them carrying us all this way just to be eaten."

"Well, that's too bad, isn't it?" snapped Handen. "They're horses and that's what they do—they carry stuff until they can't carry anymore and then they get eaten. It's not much of a life, but it's better than our prospects if the Regulators catch up with us."

The two remained silent in the early morning dark. The tension of their journey had strained the temperament of both travelers, testing their patience and camaraderie to the very limit. The rhythmic rasping of Wynona was the only sound to be heard.

Handen broke the silence. "Do you want to have a try at lighting this fire, then?"

Bip looked at the rubble, a mixture of half-damp wood and leaves that would take a lot of heat to dry out and burn. They had been taking opportunities wherever possible to try to develop Bip's psyentific knack to a more predictable and serviceable level throughout the journey, and various forest fires and mysterious igloos lay scattered in their wake as evidence of the fact. Currently, Bip's goal for self-improvement was to light a controlled fire using his knack. The emphasis had been on the word controlled.

Bip looked at the pile of barely combustible debris until he pinpointed a likely molecular source of kindling. He concentrated on making the molecules dance, remembering, as he always did in these circumstances, the voice of his teacher, Glimton...

You'll never amount to anything, you worthless bag of snot!

There was a satisfying *whoomph* as the rubble pile sparked into a huge bonfire. The blast had been big enough to singe the Kaneqian's eyelashes through his glasses, but not so big, he was pleased to see, as to demolish half of the campsite, as his last attempt had.

"You're improving," said Handen, wiping soot from his face. "Still a long way to go, but you're getting there."

Bip grinned. It was the closest thing to praise he had received in regards to his psyentific abilities in a long time.

The two fugitives sat, appreciating the warmth of the fire in the morning chill, their moods lightening at the small victory. Eventually, Handen constructed a spit from a few handy twigs and began roasting a game bird he had felled the previous day. The smell of cooking meat was tantalizing after a hard day's ride.

After a while, they ate, then lay back in the satisfied glow of a meal well done.

"Where do you suppose it comes from?" said Bip, breaking the comfortable silence. "The psyence, I mean?"

"How do you mean?" said Handen.

"Well, from what I've been told and what I've seen, Berschites, the people of this planet, can't do it. My friend Azron thought it was something called magic."

"Ah, magic," said Handen. "Magic is a word used by the ignorant to explain what they don't understand. It's just a term used by people who haven't got all the facts yet. Or sometimes a word used by those with knowledge who want to keep others in the dark. Charlatans or showmen."

"Just tricks, you mean?" said Bip.

"Yes," replied Handen, "and no. Your gift—the way you just started that fire—some would call it magic because they can't explain it. Doesn't mean it was a trick."

"So magic is kind of a question that hasn't been answered yet?" said Bip thoughtfully.

"Or an answer you haven't questioned. The fact is that what you call psyence, and what was called equating in my time, doesn't come from any sort of mystical force. It's a physical trait, like wings on a bird or horns on a jabberwocky."

Bip nodded. The adventurer continued his explanation.

"The Clarions, or the Kaneqians if you prefer, can see the very structure of the world in front of them, can view the material energy plane, and by seeing it, they can connect with it and influence it. We're all made of energy at a sub-molecular level, after all. So, it's not a trick; it's just a matter of balancing a physical-energy equation that's already there in a different way, through a hereditary relationship with the world around us."

Bip nodded. Though he had heard similar explanations of psyence throughout his education and training, Handen's approach was refreshingly pragmatic.

"But magic," said Handen, shaking his head slightly. "I've seen some unusual things on this world—sorcerers and wizards and warriors of superhuman ability. But those abilities were learned and mastered by ordinary men through terrestrial means. There is no magic, only secrets we haven't found."

Bip lay back, gazing at the stars through a hole in the farmhouse roof. "I understand that psyence is a hereditary trait, but where do you suppose it comes from? I know we're born with it, but why?" he said.

Handen lay back, too, feeling as relaxed as he ever would while they were still fleeing the law.

"That's a good question," he said, after a while. "I wish you could have met Julius; he was the man for this sort of talk. It was never my thing, really—I was more about blowing stuff up to tell the truth—but Julius would go on for ages about the Clarions' origins." Handen screwed up his eyes in recollection. "He figured that life evolves to the star it's born to, that sometimes life can find a way to succeed in what you and I might consider the most unlikely of places. He believed we were descended from a race that grew where the universal rules were slightly different, where the stars were…what's the word he used? I can't remember, but the stars were different. He thinks that where we came from, where we originally came from, the matter there was less…asserted. One thing wasn't always the other, if you know what I mean. Everything was kind of linked, but in an obvious way, a way you could manipulate. See? He thought that psyence was a legacy of distant ancestors who existed integrally with the world around them. Do you understand?" Handen, lost in his retelling of his long-since-gone captain's theories, suddenly became aware that the conversation had become a bit one-sided.

"Do you see what I'm getting at?" he said. A loud snore was his only response. Handen smiled and rolled onto his side, feeling sleep creeping up on him with sluggish seduction.

That night he dreamed of the worlds he had left behind—and the friends, too many to count, whom he would never see again.

4

The Bone Desert

They had ridden hard for a month. The populated areas of the Panthalus province and the grassy dales thereafter were far behind them. They had not seen another living soul since they had last traded with a gruff old farmer just before the Quiet Mountains. Happily (at least for Bip,) both Wynona and Gertrude had made it as far as the farm and had been traded for younger, fresher mounts. It was these mounts that had led the cart through the stillness of the Quiet Mountains, so named with good reason, for not a creature stirred, and only the rattle of the cart's wheels on stony ground broke the engulfing silence.

Cowed by the constant hush, Bip and Handen made camp without a word, afraid that to make a noise would disturb the peace of the eerie stone hills and bring the attention of any predators that lurked in the mists.

It was said that there were mountain trolls and hill giants that stalked the Quiet Mountains at night. Handen, though, was outwardly dismissive of the possibilities of proto-beings living in the hills, dismissing the stories as superstition and rumor. However, when night fell, and the eerie quiet developed a personal and dangerous quality, the two fugitives found themselves keeping a more rigid watch than usual, expecting at any moment to see the moon blotted out by huge, marauding silhouettes.

They were glad to leave the mountains behind, though there were still no signs of any settlements or even much wildlife in the lands they traveled thereafter. The fugitives simply rode on as the land around them became more desolate and the temperature increased by the day until the heat became nearly unbearable. Grass gave way to hard mud. Mud gave way to shale. The days plodded by, shuffling their feet as they went.

The Bone Desert sneaked up on them. It shouldn't have been able to, but the steep incline Handen and Bip had been riding up was so gradual that they barely realized it was there, so they were shocked to suddenly find themselves atop a cliff face overlooking a wide ocean of sand.

"Wow," breathed Bip.

"Don't be intimidated," said Handen. "It's only a few days ride to the Nastre Kingdom, then we turn east, and it's another few days ride back to more hospitable territory."

"The Nastre Kingdom…do you think we'll be able to get more supplies there?" said Bip.

"As a matter of fact, I'm counting on it. We won't be able to take the cart over this terrain, so we'll be packing essentials only from here on in."

"But we're wanted men," said Bip. "Aren't we taking a bit of a risk assuming we can restock at Nastre?"

"A slight risk," said Handen, wobbling his hand from side to side as he scanned the sandy horizon. "But a calculated one. The Nastre Kingdom is officially part of the Empire, but it's too remote to warrant much personal attention. They pledge allegiance, pay taxes and the odd tribute when necessary, but they still operate as an independent kingdom, with their own customs and even laws sometimes. I don't think word of us will have got there yet, and if it has, I don't think we'll be regarded as a major concern either way. Nastre is the closest were going to get to a civilized no-man's land in the whole of Regalious."

Bip looked at his friend. "You seem to know a lot about Nastre."

"I picked it up in Sloe," said the immortal dismissively, referring to one of the dwindling outposts they had stopped at on their travels. Handen was good at picking up information without appearing suspiciously curious.

Bip followed Handen's gaze out toward the gently shifting desert. The sun was already beginning to feel horribly oppressive. The former Hostilities Advisor seemed lost in contemplation, his usually calculating features smoothed over with a hint of melancholy. As they had traveled, Handen had discovered that, particularly when traveling in a place he had been to before, fragments of his lost memories would become astonishingly and suddenly clear. Now, as he looked over the empty plain of sand before him, images of a city skyline on the horizon niggled at his brain.

"You know," Handen said, "the last time I was here, Nastre was a huge and powerful country. Cities all over the place, with temples and museums you would have strained your neck to take in. Now it's no more than an outpost for the Empire, clinging on to the old ways like a senile war veteran."

"What do you suppose happened?" said Bip.

"The Empire, presumably," muttered Handen. "My, how things have changed."

The two travelers stood for a while, staring out into the lonely-looking sands. "So we ride due south?" said Bip eventually.

"Yep," said Handen. "Due south to Nastre."

They packed what they needed onto their mounts and headed down the cliff slope and into the burning sands.

THE HEAT HAD BEEN, frankly, unreasonable. It had been impossible to travel when the sun was high in the sky, so Handen and Bip had opted to travel only early mornings, late afternoons, and throughout the evenings. Ultimately, this meant that their arrival at Nastre would be delayed by a day or so. Handen cursed himself for underestimating how much of a chore crossing even a small part of the Bone Desert would be. They trudged along, the horses sweating and stinking in the relentless sun, their bodies slick with sticky moisture. The heat radiated from the sand, offering no reprieve from the baking desert sky.

At their first rest stop, Bip had tried to alleviate some of the discomfort by trying to purposefully, rather than accidentally, equate an igloo so that they might cool off for a while. He failed, constructing instead an impressively large but ultimately useless sandcastle. So, on they went, further toward the wavering horizons. Their only relief came with the double-edged sword of nightfall, which, while dispelling the heat of the day, brought with it a deadly chill.

As the desert moon turned gold sands to silver, Handen and Bip sat huddled under a blanket. They kept close to the small fire they had managed to make from the already dwindling supply of wood, though it did little to deter the biting desert breeze, which, as an added bonus, would continually slap them with erratic drifts of coarse sand. The stars hung like icicles in the sky, and Bip looked up into an oblivion that seemed a little colder than usual.

"Hard to believe they're all suns," he said, his breath freezing in the air.

Handen looked up but didn't say anything.

"I mean, that there could be a world like ours for every star in the sky," continued Bip.

"It's not that special, really," said Handen. "It's nice and all, but when you've been to as many planets as I have, they all start to look a bit similar. Now and again one'll throw you something interesting and unexpected, but you'd be surprised how closely beings in the same universe evolve, on the whole."

"If that's your attitude, then why were you—and the Caretakers for that matter—so intent on saving Bersch from destruction? It's only one planet, one civilization of many, I suppose?" said Bip, his teeth chattering in the cold.

Handen turned his stony gaze to his companion. "The destiny of every planet is important. We believe that every race deserves the chance to mature to a point where it can survive outside interferences on its own. It doesn't mean that any one planet is any more particularly special than another. They all have their good points, bad points, similarities, differences." Handen shrugged, his shoulders shivering as he did so.

Bip smiled to himself. "They're like children," he muttered. "The planets are like children and you lot are like babysitters." He laughed. Handen joined in.

"That's as good a comparison as any," said the former Hostilities Advisor.

"And now this planet, the one we're standing on, is going to be wiped out by an unknown astral disaster…" Bip said reflectively.

Handen shook his head. "Not unknown," he said. "The Clarions have been tracking the progress of the disaster for thousands of years. We know exactly what it is."

"Then what is it?" said Bip, shocked. This was all news to him.

"It's a cluster of ancient devastation weapons, warped and mutated by countless aeons of multiple radiation exposure, launched by a species who were particularly adept at blowing the crap out of things, and rather unimaginatively christened the 'Massive Ball of Death.' When it hits Bersch, there will be nothing left but poisoned rubble. If that."

Bip stared into the sky, envisioning a world of fire. "Why would someone do that?" he breathed.

Handen chuckled. "The funny thing is that the species who launched the weapons didn't even think about the possibility of affecting other races. They were quite confident that they were alone in their universe. Shows what they knew." Handen snorted a quick derisive laugh. "The reason the cluster is heading this way is pure coincidence—adverse randominity."

"The Discordance?" said Bip. He shuddered, recalling the metal grin of the red-skinned troublemaker, Mr. Random.

"That's right." Handen nodded. "They influence things, affect things. Things that would be better left alone. We had the technology to detect their actions from back on the homeworlds—that was how we tracked the disaster—we could tell when there was outside interference in the expected course of events."

"How?" said Bip.

Handen frowned in remembrance. "Ripples in causality. We had machines that could detect them, like seismographs can detect earthquakes. Let us know where the Discordance were messing around with things."

Bip thought back to his own encounter with Mr. Random. "Have you ever seen one of them?" he asked. "One of the Discordance, I mean."

Handen shook his head. "They've never warranted my personal attention. Me? I'm mostly just good for fighting, and the Discordance are an enemy that can't be fought, at least not with any weapon I can use. See, they belong in a different dimension to ours, and they can only affect things mentally in our world, not physically. They're like mischievous ghosts, I suppose—they influence things with weaker minds, twist the will of others, and bring bad luck wherever they can. And they worship chaos totally." Handen grinned suddenly. "They worship chaos, but they use surprisingly well-organized methods to achieve it. Paradoxical. Tells us a bit about their character."

Bip nodded. "You've never met one, then?"

"No," said Handen. "As I said, we can't fight them, and they can't fight us…at least not directly. All we do is try to stay one step ahead of them and clean up their mess whenever possible."

"Is that what you're doing here at Bersch? Cleaning up mess?"

"In a manner of speaking, yes. Though we didn't do a very good job of it in retrospect." Handen gave a grim smile. "Now save your breath—we've got a long, cold night ahead of us and a long, hot day tomorrow."

They huddled together against the night's chill, knowing that reprieve would only come in a polar-opposite form of torture.

Slowly, the cold making him groggy, Bip began to fall asleep.

He was never sure whether he'd actually fallen asleep or not, he was only aware, suddenly, of a familiar yet still unsettling feeling. The feeling that something was amiss, that things weren't quite right. A panicky suspicion bubbled up in Bip's mind and, sure enough, was confirmed almost immediately.

"Speak of the devil, and he shall appear," crooned an elegant voice.

Bip looked up to see Mr. Random squatting by the dying remains of the campfire. He quickly looked to see if Handen was awake. The adventurer lay sleeping, his brow furrowed as though dreaming of problems.

"Wouldn't be able to see me even if he were awake," said Mr. Random, poking at an ember with his fiendishly long fingers. "I wouldn't want to spoil our special relationship, Bip. After all, two's company..." The apparition grinned his terrible metal grin.

"What do you want this time?" said Bip.

"Just to chat, Bippy, just to chat," said Mr. Random chirpily. "You know, I was a little annoyed. Right now, you're supposed to be rotting in a cell somewhere, but instead, here you are. And with Mr. Strike as well, it seems. What are the chances?"

Bip frowned. "You know Handen?"

Random's seemingly permanent smirk left his features, replaced by a snarling rage that made Bip unconsciously shuffle backward. "Know him?" he said. "I spent the best part of a millennium trying to kill him! The stubborn git refuses to die! And now here he is, back again. I don't think you realize how much that ticks me off, Bippy-boy." Random calmed down and sat back on his haunches. "Not that it will matter," he said. "You're running a bit too late to stop us now."

"We can still make it," said Bip. "We still have time."

"I'll stop you," said Random. "Just like I stopped the others before you."

Now it was Bip's turn to smirk. He gestured toward the sleeping Handen. "You didn't stop all of us," he said.

Mr. Random's features went cold, his metal grin disappearing. "One fish through the net, that's all. I stopped the others. Stopped them dead. I stopped your father!" Bip reeled. He had dealt with the conclusion that his father had met a sticky end a long time ago, but to hear it confirmed was like being kicked in the stomach. Mr. Random's metal smile snaked back across his features. "Yes, that's right," he said.

"He was a tough one, was your old man. He made it all the way to the Cold Ocean before having an unfortunate run-in with a wavesnake!"

"Shut up!" shouted Bip. "Shut up or I'll—"

"You'll what?" said Random. "You can't touch me, and you know it!"

"Maybe not," spat Bip. "But I can ignore you."

Affronted, Mr. Random gaped stupidly as Bip rolled over and hunkered down on his sleeping mat.

"You'll never make it, you know," he said. "Even with Mr. Strike helping you, I'll still stop you. Stop you dead!"

"I'm not listening," said Bip.

"You can't ignore me, you worm! I hold power you couldn't possibly understand! I have meddled with the fate of galaxies! You really think a poxy maggot like you can stand in my way?" Mr. Random was screeching now, standing up to bellow at Bip's slumped form.

"Could have sworn I heard something," mumbled Bip. "Must have been the wind…"

Mr. Random gaped and flustered for a moment, then shut his mouth with a formal click and stalked off into the desert night. Bip relaxed and sighed heavily with relief. There must have been five minutes of quiet and then—just as Bip was settling into a shallow sleep—he heard a crooning voice begin to sing by his ear.

"I know a song that will get on your nerves, get on your nerves, get on your nerves…"

Bip groaned and put his rucksack over his ears.

"…get, get, get on your nerves."

THE TRAVELERS AWOKE to the incessant glare of the rising sun. The cold of the previous night quickly melted away, promising a few moments of pleasant warmth before the heat became unbearable once again. Without a word, Bip and Handen shouldered their packs and began to lead their mounts, stretching their legs, and saving some of the horses' energy for when the sun was higher in the sky. They walked for a while in silence, Bip trying unsuccessfully to blink the sleep from his eyes, Handen staring hard at the horizon with his usual calculating gaze.

"Sleep well last night?" asked the adventurer conversationally.

"No," said Bip, deciding not to tell Handen about his conversation with Mr. Random. After all, what good would it do? Right now, Handen was focused entirely on getting to Argustin safely and in good time. Distracting him with more nebulous worries might prove a hindrance—and was probably just what Mr. Random wanted. Bip decided to bear his fear and doubt on his own shoulders. *Two's company*, he thought, and grinned mirthlessly.

"The cold, right? Kept me awake for a while, too," said Handen, returning his gaze to the horizon.

"That's right," mumbled Bip, and yawned long and wide. He wondered why Mr. Random had never appeared to Handen, and whether he had ever appeared to any of the other volunteers, in the flesh, so to speak. He doubted it somehow. He assumed that Mr. Random was only appearing now because there was so little time left before the Massive Ball of Death hit. He was probably just making sure everything was going to go right for him.

Bastard, thought Bip distractedly.

They walked for half the morning, mounting up for a few hours before noon when the sun reached its zenith, then rested in the baking sand for what seemed like far too long. They wore clothing soaked in water from the worryingly low supplies in their skins, draped over their heads to ward off sunstroke and burn. Handen reflected that they would have to reach Nastre soon—a day in the Bone Desert without water was not an inviting prospect.

As the sun relented slightly in the afternoon, the travelers mounted up again and made as good a pace as possible on the panting horses. They traversed dune after shimmering dune, the sky a hard, bright opal above them.

As they rode, Bip pointed hopefully at what had looked like buildings off to their south. Handen had stared for a while at the wavering mirage of the horizon, shielding his eyes from the sun.

"Is it the city?" said Bip.

Handen stared for a little while longer before turning to his companion. "No," he said. "Concentrate on the buildings. Tell me what you see."

Bip squinted for a long time. "They're triangles?" he ventured.

"Pyramids, actually," said Handen. "They're not houses; they're tombs. The Nastren people used to bury their dead kings in huge stone pyramids."

"Why?"

Handen shrugged. "Why do we mark graves at all? I suppose it was just a way of showing how revered the king was."

Bip stared hard at the distant bumps.

"Don't let distance fool you," said Handen. "Those things are massive."

"Been close to one before, have you?" asked Bip.

"Yeah," said Handen, smiling faintly. "Kind of nice seeing something older than I am. Come on, let's get a move on."

At night they camped again, this time able to bolster their small amount of wood with some tough, dry shrubs found in a cluster of rocks. The rocks made good shelter from the cold evening wind and their sleep was more comfortable than the previous nights.

Dawn came once more, and the two fugitives upped their pace, rested as they were from the previous night. It was late afternoon when a faint glimmer on the horizon hinted at civilization.

"Just as well, really," Handen commented, rattling his empty waterskin.

They reached a small village just before nightfall, a settlement of a little over twenty stone hovels, surrounded by small ranches where camels and horses chewed the dry sandgrass with an animal patience as wide as the horizon. Thankfully they had been able to refill their water supplies from a stone well, drawing the ground-cooled water whilst silent locals watched them suspiciously, eyes piercing brightly from identically desert-baked faces. Handen realized that it must have been some time since outsiders had ridden through the village, and that their clothing and features probably seemed quite alien to the people there. So that night, they camped on the outskirts of the settlement—close enough to provide some shelter from the winds, but not so close as to make the villagers wary.

Handen was busily tearing at some white cloth he had managed to trade for before night had fallen. He was trying to construct an imitation of the white robes the Nastre people wore, both because they were convenient for the weather conditions and also because they could disguise their faces, meaning that with any luck, they wouldn't draw attention to themselves as they entered Nastre city.

Their meat supply now depleted, Bip made a thick soup out of the last of their vegetable stock, adding some of their precious store of salt to create a thick, nourishing, and tasty meal. They ate with gusto —it would be the last solid meal they would have until they were able to trade for more food or were able to hunt for it, an option that had become increasingly unlikely in a desert seemingly devoid of wildlife.

That night they slept soundly and were up with the rising of the sun, refilling their waterskins, donning their robes, and heading east before any of the villagers had begun their day.

THEY TRAVELED for another day before reaching the outer walls of Nastre, their progress made easier by the discovery of a road that, while in a state of grievous disrepair, was better traveling than the sand dunes that surrounded it. The city walls, large undecorated constructions the color of old dust, had obviously been built in a time when invasion had been a serious threat. Now they stood unmanned, with nothing to watch for but the occasional sandstorm. The main gates were heavy, wooden, and towered the full height of the walls but, judging from the amount of sand that had piled up around their bases, had remained opened and unused for a very long time.

Only two watchmen stood guard over the entrance to the city proper. They too wore the desert robes common to Nastre, though they kept their muscular arms bare and wore large, curved watoki blades across the front of their waists. As the travelers came near, one of the guards signaled for them to stop and then approached with the nonchalant gait of one who is employed to detect trouble and doesn't expect to find any.

"Purpose of visit?" he said. His accent, more used to the trade speak used by the varying dialects of Nastre, rolled uncertainly around the Imperial vowels. Handen realized that the desert robes had done very little to disguise his foreign features. He quickly recounted the lie he and Bip had formulated a few nights ago, that they were business representatives from Panthalus come to secure a trade link with a spice merchant. If the guard had any doubts about the legitimacy of their story, they were quickly obliterated by the sight of Bip's gold supply—diminished but still impressive.

The two fugitives were waved through, and the watchman went back to staring blankly at the empty desert road before them.

Considering the perimeter of the city walls, the city itself seemed rather bare in comparison. It was some minutes before Handen and Bip came across any signs of civilization greater than the village they had already encountered, though a large domed palace on the horizon indicated where the hub of the city's populace was to be found.

They followed the main road toward the palace, and gradually the noise and activity began to increase around them. The small, dilapidated hut-like lodgings gave way to houses of stone and wood, though these too were shoddy affairs. Tented dwellings that seemed to have been constructed with little or no planning or forethought took up much of the space between the more permanent-looking buildings. People of all ages, all bearing the dark skin and bright white eyes Bip had come to associate with the Nastre Kingdom, ran about seemingly with more haste than purpose. More than a few stopped to stare openly at the strangers.

The noise around them gradually ascended into the cacophony Bip had begun to expect from a city, though this time the shouting voices were in a language he had never heard before. The effect was disconcerting for the traveler, and he felt more alienated than he had since the beginning of his journey. Handen, of course, took it in his stride.

A small chip from Bip's lump of gold had been enough to secure their horses indefinitely in a livery stable, so Handen and Bip wandered into what appeared to be the market sector to start the arduous process of securing enough supplies for their journey east. Handen, having no memory of any of the Nastre dialects, and the various merchants proffering only blank stares when addressed in Imperial, was forced to resort to the age-old international communication method of pointing and gesturing until the wanted item and was finally secured and the correct amount paid. Needless to say, the process was long and frustrating.

Eventually, with food and fuel and a few useful items purchased and stowed, the two doomsayers relaxed in the tented shade of a Nastren coffee house. Bip looked down at his coffee, which was dark, spicy-smelling, and apparently came with neither milk nor sugar. He took a sip. It wasn't bad.

"So, what now?" he said.

Handen sipped thoughtfully for a moment before replying. "Well, I thought we could lay low for a while."

Bip, who had been praying that Handen would say something to that effect, still voiced his concern. "Isn't that a little bit risky?"

"A little," agreed Handen. "But we need to rest the mounts, and it'll be a long time before we have anywhere as safe as Nastre to get our heads down. I think we should take this opportunity to kick back for a few days."

Bip looked around and leaned over conspiratorially. "We're not exactly inconspicuous, though, are we?"

He had a point. In the entire city, Bip and Handen had seen no one else with pale skin, and though the desert robes hid their identities from a distance, on close inspection, it was easy to see that they were not natives.

"I wouldn't worry too much," said Handen, stretching. "It's a crowded city. We're likely to spot a posse of Regulators before they spot us. And remember there's a very good chance that they won't even consider risking the Bone Desert."

"Really?"

"Just relax," said Handen. "If we don't rest, we'll exhaust ourselves before we reach the capital, and then we won't be any good to anyone. And I, for one, am looking forward to sleeping in a bed tonight." He drained the rest of his coffee. "Now," he said. "How about we hire a room out in an inn somewhere and sleep for about…oh, I don't know, forever?"

Bip grinned. "Sounds good."

BIP STEPPED ONCE MORE into the hurly-burly of the market quarter, blinking happily in the sunshine. It had been a long time since he had felt so rested, and not since the airboat had he slept so much in one sitting. Handen had leniently allocated some of the tight travel budget to a session in the local bathhouse, where Bip had had his first decent wash in months, floating happily while the various twinges and cramps courtesy of sleeping rough for so long had slowly dissipated into the hot, scented waters. Afterward, they had checked into a local inn and had simply spent an entire day doing nothing but sleeping and eating.

Now, on their second morning in the desert city, the fugitives were preparing to leave. Handen had wanted to take one last wander around to see if he could garner any useful information and, knowing that Bip might have proven a liability, he had sent the Kaneqian out on his own to pick up a few non-essential supplies. And so, with plenty of time until their agreed rendezvous, Bip took a leisurely stroll through the endless tents of market stalls.

He wandered lazily.

Lulled by the midday heat into a dreamy state, he paid little attention to the world around him, so he did not notice that the accustomed curiosity of the locals had taken on a more apprehensive quality. As he meandered obliviously through the streets, eyes followed and people whispered. Shoppers walking his way swerved carefully to avoid him, so that Bip walked in a small island of calm in the otherwise hectic scrum of the marketplace. Still heedless enough to the atmosphere around him to be whistling cheerfully, Bip approached a spice merchant's shack and began to browse the goods.

The merchant made to approach Bip with the aggressive friendliness typical of the Nastre salesman, but before he could launch into his usual chatter, he performed an almost comical double-take, his eyes widening in his aged face. He began to babble in the clipped and puzzling Nastre vernacular and make frantic gestures at the doomsayer.

Bip frowned, trying to guess what the shopkeeper was attempting to communicate.

"I'm Just Browsing, Thanks!" he said, talking loudly and clearly as if this could compensate for speaking an entirely incompatible language.

The shopkeeper continued his aggressive gesturing and eventually reached for the drawstrings that held the tent flaps of his stall open. With a sharp slapping noise, the tent-shop closed up, cutting off the still-babbling voice of the shopkeeper.

Bip stood back for a moment, frowning in puzzlement. It was then that he saw the sign on the outside of the tent. The paper was bright, obviously freshly put up, and the words were, of course, indecipherable. The pictures, however, two quite good artists' renditions of Bip and Handen, were immediately clear.

Realizing the implications, Bip swallowed hard and made to go and find his fellow fugitive. He turned around to find his retreat barred by the tips of two watoki blades leveled at his throat. The glinting eyes of two guardsmen regarded him solemnly from behind their identical desert robes.

"Ah..." said Bip, and wondered what to do next.

5

You Can't Keep a Bad Man Down

The Last Palace used to be just one of the many grandiosely domed and extravagantly spired palaces that had formerly been a frequent, almost common sight across the once great kingdom of Nastre. Now, however, it was the only one remaining in a land that been largely reclaimed by the ever-pressing advance of the Bone Desert. Only a few of the oldest citizens of the desert kingdom remembered the days when the palace had been called by its true name, a name that had reflected the might and majesty that inspire and conceive such architectural triumphs. Now it was known only as the Last Palace.

It was central to the city around it, and much of its grounds had been overtaken by a sprawl of shops and settlements. The building had been depleted since its glory days, whole wings had been demolished and recycled by a city that could no longer afford the tax to maintain it. The Last Palace was symbolic of the fall of the Nastre Kingdom—a ghost of a more prosperous time. A grand history withered by a modernizing world. A dust-colored grave for the pride, might and arrogance that had flavored the city so many centuries ago.

The king still resided in the palace, as was expected of the ruler of the desert tribes. Though in truth, he was no more than a mayoral figurehead in the city, emerging from the ill-swept corridors now and then to issue royal decrees to nostalgic subjects who would applaud loudly and promptly forget what had been said. Since the fall of Nastre to the Empire, the king was little more than a blue-blooded mascot. He had no more real authority in the affairs of Nastre than the Imperially-appointed sheriff, though he still wore the golden robes and mask of his godlike ancestors as he delivered his pointless sermons to a broken people.

One of the few, purely ceremonial responsibilities the king enjoyed was the judging and sentencing of perpetrators...providing said perpetrators had already been found guilty by the sheriff or another Empire official. And so it seemed Bip was going to meet the king of Nastre.

The corridor Bip waited in was similar to the one he had sat in at the court of Panthalus so many weeks ago, though this was more stylishly constructed, with huge sand-yellow bricks on which famous battles from Nastren history were depicted in faded, intricate paintings. Another happy improvement on his pre-court experience in Panthalus lay with his chaperones; the two silent guardsmen who sat on either side of him on the wooden bench were infinitely preferable company to the loathsome and odorsome Blungkit.

All of a sudden, wooden doors were flung open with a crash that wrecked the stone silence of the corridor. Handen was marched across to the bench by a group of guards and shoved into a sitting position. His hands were tied behind his back and, unlike Bip, who had merely been escorted by the two guards he was sitting with, Handen was surrounded by a dozen or so, all with weapons drawn and ready. Quite a few of the Nastrens were sporting dark bruises on the visible parts of their bodies, and Bip guessed that many of the original arresting party had not made it as far as the temple.

Handen himself had a huge black eye and a deep cut on his forehead, both of which, of course, would begin to heal at any moment.

Bip's heart sank. Some keen and loyal part of his mind had been relying on the former Hostilities Advisor for his rescue. "They got you, too," he stated, glumly.

"You can't win them all," replied Handen. He sounded nonchalant, though his anger was betrayed by the dangerous glint in his eye.

"How do you suppose they found out about us?" said Bip.

"Well, I doubt we were beaten here by anyone tracking us from Panthalus," said Handen. "My best guess is that there's a Regulator station close to the Bone Desert with a telegram receiver. They must have sent a messenger to the city either just as we were arriving or a little before." The adventurer wiggled his lips, trying to scratch his nose without using his hands.

"It all seems a bit much," said Bip, gloomily. "Why are they going to so much trouble to capture us? We're only two men!"

"You're right," replied Handen. "It does seem a bit excessive seeing as we haven't killed anyone or stolen anything. My best bet is that your friend Blungkit has friends in high places."

Bip tried to think of the repugnant Blungkit swanning around in the high society circles of the Panthalus province. The image did not come easily. He shared his doubts with Handen.

"Fair enough," the adventurer said. "Either way, it doesn't matter to us now. All we have to worry about now is whether the Nastre justices will hand us over to Empire representatives or deal with us themselves."

"What difference will it make?" said Bip.

"Well," said Handen, still trying vainly to scratch his nose, "if we're handed over to the Empire, we could be detained for as long as it takes to send an escort. If not, we could be hanged tomorrow."

"Oh," said Bip, trying not to sound as defeated as he felt. A sudden spark of hope briefly lit within him. "Surely if we're detained, there's a possibility of escape?" he said.

Handen's features remained serious and indifferent. "I'd like to say something like 'there's never been a prison built that could hold me,' but seeing as I was locked up for the last five hundred years, I think that would be a rather bogus assertion."

Bip slumped, the brief spark in of hope squashed mercilessly. "So, what you're saying is, we're buggered?"

"That about sums it up," Handen agreed. "If they put us under a light guard—which they won't—or if we had a contact in the city—which we don't—we might stand a chance, but..." Handen left the rest of the sentence unsaid, merely shrugging his shoulders.

"Oh, great," Bip said. "Just great. We're going to die!" He stopped and thought about it. "Well...I'm going to die. You can't, can you?"

"Lucky me," said Handen, sarcastically. "With any luck, I'll just be locked up for another eternity or so."

THE PALACE THRONE room was the largest room Bip had seen since his time in the Dome. It was illuminated by huge windows built high toward the ceiling, and the daylight that filtered through was reflected from various strategically and aesthetically placed mirrors, meaning it was nearly as bright as the streets outside. The room was built from the same yellowy sandstone blocks as the rest of the palace, though here they looked freshly scrubbed. Large and exquisite tapestries hung from the walls and plush red rugs covered the floor leading to a large and ridiculously ornate golden throne. Someone had taken great pains to ensure that the throne room of the Last Palace was restored to the majesty of Nastre's worthy history. Looking at this room, one could almost forget the decay and disrepair that riddled the rest of the palace.

Bip and Handen were marched down the length of the room toward the throne, where a thin figure in a golden mask sat waiting for them. Bip noticed, with a feeling like some illegitimate son of jealousy, that all the guards' attention (not to mention their weapons) were focused entirely on Handen.

They were taken before the throne, where a herald heralded them in words they couldn't understand. The various courtiers in the throne room stood in respectful silence while the king looked down at them. The king was a tall figure, though any other physical observation of him was denied. His shimmering gold-colored robes completely hid his frame, and the golden mask—which to Bip's mind resembled the face of a toddler who had just successfully stolen a biscuit—covered his head completely.

The man who stood on the king's right, however, had no such finery. He wore only a long-coated gray uniform that, while subtly altered from those Bip had seen in Panthalus and the Free Countries, was recognizable as the Regulator uniform. Evidently this man, with his insidious moustache and watchful, amused eyes, was the sheriff.

"Welcome, my friends!" said the sheriff, and Handen pegged him immediately—anyone who crafts your doom and still insists on calling you "friend," he later told Bip, is a man that can be trusted about as far as you can throw him.

"What a time the Empire has had trying to keep up with you! Most distressed, they have been!" Though the sheriff's Imperial was impeccable, the rich timbre of his desert birth still reverberated through his sentences with a syrupy bass. "Imagine my surprise when, having just been informed of your escape, my informers told of two white-skinned strangers wandering around." The sheriff laughed a deep and unpleasant laugh. The golden mask of the king turned slightly at the sound, but nothing was said.

"Is that what we're to be tried for?" said Handen. "Escape?"

"Amongst other things," the sheriff purred. "Our lord Emperor Draegul (may snakes infest the underwear drawers of his enemies) has taken a particular interest in you."

Bip and Handen shared a brief glance, the same question running through their minds: why would the Emperor be interested in two escaped mental patients?

"And now," continued the sheriff, "it gives me enormous pleasure to turn to our great and good king to offer judgment on your souls."

The king's golden mask seemed to look in all directions, as though abruptly awoken from a catnap. He raised a hand from beneath his robes and seemed as if he were about to say something. Before he could, however, the sheriff began speaking again.

"For the crimes of escaping Imperial justice, for the brutal assault of a respected Regulator, for impersonating sane people, and for, no doubt, countless thefts and murders we have yet to find evidence of, you are to be detained until the relevant Imperial authorities can arrive and exact justice." The echoes of the sheriff's words were quickly captured and smothered by the thick silence of the throne room.

"Funny," Bip said. "The king managed to say all that without moving his mouth."

The sheriff's expression of amused authority was replaced in a flash by a broiling outrage. "Silence, you scum!" he roared. "The king does not need to soil his holy tongue with unnecessary platitudes for worthless dunebug dung like yourselves. His wisdom has been made known through my person!"

The king's golden mask tilted slightly to one side. He seemed to shrug under the heavy folds of his robes. The sheriff calmed himself before speaking again.

"And now, His Majesty is tired from his duties and wishes to retire for the day. Have these two criminals clapped in irons and detained in the royal dungeons."

IT COULD BE ARGUED that the royal dungeons were another part of the Last Palace where great care and attention had been taken to ensure the glory days were preserved and painstakingly restored. However, how much care and attention it actually took to ensure a room remained a slime-covered, dust-ridden tomb of hopelessness was debatable. Certainly the underground dungeons served the purpose they had originally been designed for, which was to be unpleasant and inescapable. If despair had a smell, then these dungeons stank of it.

Bip and Handen had been manacled to the walls, just in case several feet of brick tempered by time into something hard and organic posed too much of an escape opportunity. Handen experimented with the rusted but still thick chains, leaning all his weight and putting all his muscle into trying to dislodge the manacles from the wall, but his efforts were in vain. The manacles held fast.

"Sorry, Bip," the adventurer said. "I don't think we'll be getting out of here in a hurry."

"Damn," said Bip.

They hung in silence for a while, looking about the slick-walled prison around them.

"And you're sure you can't see any loose bricks or handy drains?" said Bip eventually.

"You mean since we looked last time? No."

"Okay, okay," Bip said testily. "I just thought we might have missed something. Or something…"

"You know," said Handen thoughtfully, "it's always struck me as strange that there seems to be this odd romantic belief going around that jails are easily escapable, somehow." He looked around at the solid-stone walls and the small but thick wooden door. "When, clearly, the very nature of a prison is to make sure you can't escape."

The two prisoners hung around. It was all they could do, really.

"Any luck with your psyence?" Handen said after a while.

"No, no good," replied Bip. "It's really hard to concentrate when you're hanging by your wrists from the ceiling."

"Yeah, I noticed that," said Handen.

The two continued to hang, swaying slightly as the air currents were disturbed by the slamming of a door somewhere in the labyrinth of the palace's lower levels. "What we need is some kind of miracle," Bip said.

"It wouldn't go amiss, no," agreed Handen.

"Some sort of nick-of-time rescue wouldn't be too bad."

"Yeah."

"Or maybe a sudden pardon."

"Yep."

"Or possibly a huge pink dragon will come along and whisk us off to the land of happy chocolate."

"Yes, that's just as likely, really."

Bip looked over at his cellmate. "You could at least humor me, you know," he said reproachfully.

"Sorry, kid, I'm fresh out of optimism," replied the former Hostilities Advisor. After a short interval of silence, Handen looked over at the downcast face of the younger man. He sighed. "Tell you what; if an opportunity arises for a sudden and dramatic escape, you'll be the first person I tell. How's that?" he said.

Bip nodded. "It's a start."

Somewhere in the lower levels another door slammed, echoing mournfully and harassing dust-motes throughout the sepulchral passageways.

"What do you suppose that was?" said Bip.

Handen didn't answer. Despite his earlier pessimistic assertions, the survivalist part of his brain was still desperately thinking of escape scenarios. He had thought of a few, but all relied heavily on specific and unlikely circumstances and a great deal of luck. Handen, of course, had no qualms about gambling with his own life (an immortal's prerogative), but was less willing to risk the skin of his relatively innocent companion. He was shaken from his thoughts by the heavy clunk of the cell door being unlocked. The tiny wooden door swung open with a protesting creak, and two of the impassive royal guardsmen entered.

"Surely the Regulators can't be here already?" Bip said, trying unsuccessfully to keep the panic from his voice.

The guards, as expected, said nothing. Instead, they waited until a third figure had entered the room. A figure attired from head to toe in gold.

"Well, well, well," said Handen. "If it isn't His Majesty. Where's your parrot? Or are you speaking up for yourself this time?"

The king didn't answer. Instead, he made a hand signal, and the two guards left the cell, shutting the door behind them. The king stood and looked at the prisoners manacled to the wall, his golden mask glowing eerily in the half-light of the dungeon.

"If you've come to gloat, we're not interested," said Handen. "Trust me, when it comes to gloating evil tyrants, I've heard the best, so you may as well just sod off!"

The face of the king's golden mask turned to Bip. A voice came from within. "He's a bit touchy, isn't he?"

Bip frowned. Though the voice reverberated oddly in the metal of the mask, there was no mistaking the thick Port Town accent.

The king removed his mask, revealing the crooked grin of a crooked man. "Alright?" he said.

Bip's jaw hung with the rest of his body. Though his skin was now deeply tanned and his hair was a little longer, there was no mistaking the face of Azron Bezron.

"Azron?" Bip gasped, too surprised to think of anything more original.

"The one and only," said the thief, and gave a sardonic little bow.

Bip's face twitched with conflicting emotions. Finally, it settled on puzzlement.

"You're the King of Nastre?" he said.

Azron rolled his eyes. "Hardly," he scoffed "I nicked it, didn't I?"

"How can you steal a kingdom?" said Bip, struggling to keep up.

"Well, I was hanging around, minding my own business, sort of thing, and I thought I'd check out the palace. Do a bit of sightseeing, you know? So I climb through a window and there's this old geezer answering a call of nature, yeah?"

"You didn't hurt him, did you?" asked Bip, his eyes narrowing mistrustfully.

"Course not! Would I do such a thing?" Azron smiled the smile of an innocent. On his face, it looked dirty. "Anyway, I didn't have to," he continued. "The old duffer took one look at me and keeled over from a heart attack."

"So what did you do?" said Bip.

"Well, next thing I know, there's these people banging on the door asking if everything's all right. So I put on my best old man voice and tell them I'm fine, (though it's hard 'cause I don't now much Trade Speak), then, when I'm wondering how I'm going to get myself out of this one, I find these little numbers." Azron gestured to his robes and the mask in his hand. "I put 'em on, stick the geezer in the bottom of the linen cupboard, and next thing I know, everyone's calling me 'Your Majesty.' Pretty nifty, eh?"

Bip's eyes were wide with disbelief. "You've been impersonating the king?"

"Yeah, for about three days now. It's easier than you'd think. No one asks me anything important, and I just nod and wave a bit. No one's the wiser."

"Unbelievable," Bip breathed. "Miraculous, in fact. "

"Ahem," said Handen. "Isn't anyone going to introduce me?"

"Oh…how rude of me," said Bip (and Handen despaired that he actually meant it). "Azron, this is Handen. Handen, Azron."

"That's Azron Bezron Diamond Geezer (1st Class)," the thief interjected smoothly. "Port Town Union of Dodgy Fellows"

"Impressive," said Handen. "I'd shake your hand, only…" He rolled his eyes meaningfully at his manacled wrists.

"Oh yeah, of course! Best be getting you down." Azron fished in his robes for a moment and eventually retrieved a set of lock picks. "Have you free in a jiffy." He grinned.

It was the work of a moment for the thief to tamper with the manacle locks ("Heavy duty, but essentially basic," he muttered as he worked), and it wasn't long before Handen and Bip had their feet on the ground once more, massaging and rotating life back into their shoulders and wrists.

Bip stretched his back and winced as it popped audibly. "What next?" he said.

"Now we get the hell out of here before someone comes to check on you," said Azron.

"Or somebody checks the linen cupboard," Handen added.

"Ah. Yes, well. That too…"

"How will we get out of the palace? The whole place must be crawling with guards," said Bip.

Azron grinned. "Exactly." He rummaged in his robes again until he fished out two watoki blades and two of the facemasks worn by the royal guardsmen. "So no one will notice a few more! As long as we keep moving, everyone will think you two are just another couple of bodyguards."

A smile broke over Handen's face. "I'm glad to see you're so prepared."

"Always prepare for the possibility that you'll be run out of town by an angry mob, that's what my old man used to say."

"And what happened to him?" asked Bip.

"Well, he…erm…he was killed by an angry mob, actually."

The fugitives and the impostor stood in an uncomfortable silence for a moment. "Well," said Handen, eventually. "No sense standing around waiting for death when there's escaping to be done. Azron, this is your plan—you lead the way."

Azron nodded and donned his golden mask. "Let's go."

THEIR ESCAPE through the halls of the Last Palace was largely uneventful. They strode along the corridors with phony confidence while guardsmen saluted their passing. Two solitary guards wandering around the halls by themselves, perhaps, would have drawn the attention of a sharp-eyed watchman; the presence of the king, however, (or at least the king's golden mask), more or less cemented their authenticity.

There was a moment of sheer dread as they masqueraded their way to freedom, one moment that sent a cold sweat of ugly certainty across the brows of all three men. That moment was, as they hurried down a dust-licked corridor, when the sheriff rounded the corner ahead of them, unexpected and as sudden as a static shock.

Bip felt his heart beating a mad tattoo against his ribs as the Imperial man approached. He tried to look straight ahead and continue the marching gait they had fallen into. He concentrated so hard that for one ludicrous and panicky moment, he completely forgot how to walk. On the verge of stumbling and sprawling hopelessly to the floor, the Kaneqian was shocked to a sudden stop as they were hailed in the Trade Speak tongue.

The sheriff approached with his usual look of patronizing amusement, extenuated by his oily moustache, and for a moment, Bip was certain they had been discovered, expecting at any moment a contingent of the royal guard to round the corner in the sheriff's wake. His terrible certainty turned to dread confusion as the sheriff began chattering to Azron in Trade Speak, talking animatedly and cheerfully as though everything were fine. Neither Bip nor Handen could understand a word that was being said, and if Azron understood anything that was said to him, it was belied only by the way he nodded now and then and copied any hand gestures made.

There was collective sigh of relief as the sheriff walked away, laughing hard at some joke that had never made translation.

"What was he saying?" Bip whispered through the side of his mouth.

"I have no idea," replied Handen.

It was a close one but was the only time they came near to discovery before they reached the king's chambers. Once the door was safely locked behind them, Azron removed his royal attire and searched under the large, luxurious bed for his own clothes—his familiar long coat and peak-less woolen hat. Once changed, he looked under an ornate dresser and retrieved a rope that had been fashioned from silken bed sheets. Handen once again admired the forethought of a man who was always in need of an escape route. They dangled the rope from the huge bedroom window and slid down into the velvety night. Once free from the palace, sneaking into the camouflaging hubbub of the market square was an easy task.

As luck would have it, the livery master had not yet heard the rumors of fugitives in his city, so Bip and Handen's horses and equipment were still packed and ready to go. They mounted up and made ready.

Handen looked down at Azron. "I take it you're joining us?" he said.

"I don't think there's much of a future for me here once they find out the king's dead."

"Then you'd better mount up behind me," said Handen.

The thief, unpracticed in matters equine, struggled into the saddle behind the adventurer.

"We'd best not stick around," said Azron.

"I wasn't planning to," replied Handen.

"Good," muttered Azron. "I didn't understand much of what that bastard sheriff was saying, but I did pick out the words 'Emperor' and 'visit.'"

Without further talk, the three fugitives galloped east and once more into the Bone Desert.

6

Personal Attention

It was the next day. The extraordinary events of the previous night, the capture and escape of an alien and a descendant of aliens, aided by a thief who had been impersonating a dead king, seemed like day-dreamish fiction in the dawn-soaked and hardpan streets of Nastre. The citizens got on with their lives as always, greeting the much-loved apathy of inexorable routine that rose with the sun. They might have looked at the day a little differently if they had known that their king was dead and that their sheriff was as close as he had ever been to complete terror.

Sheriff Muntave Nenta stalked the corridors of the Last Palace. The look of smirking superiority had fled his face some hours ago, when he had been awoken abruptly in the early hours of the morning. Now his face was set in a grimace somewhere between panic and fury.

During the night, the king's body had been discovered by a chambermaid.

Though the maid herself had never seen the true face of the king, a dead old man stuffed into a linen cupboard was still enough to upset her a great deal. Her screams had brought the skeleton nightshift of the royal guard in less than a minute. Sheriff Muntave had been awoken not long afterward.

It hadn't taken him long to put two and two together. The body of the king was clearly not fresh, and he had likely been dead for more than a day. Muntave remembered clearly the conversation he'd had with the bearer of the golden mask before retiring to his quarters for the night. He had remembered thinking that the king, as old as he was, was a little more sedate and impassive than usual, but had pinned it on nothing more than the old fool's advancing years. Cold rage had sloshed in his stomach as he realized the huge error in judgment he had made. His anger had quickly been taken over by his dread when he'd found that the two prized prisoners had escaped. He had done nothing but stare at the empty cell for some time, as if willing himself to wake up from a stubborn and terrible nightmare. Then, with a sudden explosion of energy, he had screamed orders to any and every member of staff he encountered. The prisoners had to be bought back, and they had less than a day to do it.

When Muntave had first captured the prisoners and realized that they were valuable to the Emperor, he had wasted no time in sending a runner to the telegraph station to relay the good news to Argustin. Once the Emperor heard the news, Muntave knew it was likely a delegate would be sent to Nastre, and recognition and reward would surely follow. However, if the delegate were to travel all the way to Nastre only to be greeted by an empty cell and a flurry of excuses, then demotion or worse was a definite possibility. With this in mind, Muntave had diverted all of Nastre's meagre forces into conducting a blanket search covering the entire city and the outlying villages. Civilian militias were formed and the closest thing Nastre had seen to martial law in centuries was imposed.

All to no avail.

Eventually the sheriff acknowledged the frightening possibility that the prisoners had escaped into the Bone Desert and, with so many miles of empty country to search and the shifting sands making tracking impossible, it was unlikely they could be recaptured in time. After doing practically everything he could do, and after pacing needlessly around the palace when it became clear that nothing else could be done, Muntave sat down in his chambers and contemplated his fate. The severity of his punishment would increase with the rank of the delegate, he knew, and if a representative were sent directly from Argustin, it was likely the rank would be very high indeed.

His musings took him through the night and into the next morning. He did not sleep, only sat, thinking and hoping, barely noticing as another dawn filtered through his window.

He remembered his childhood in Gorner, a small village just outside the main city. He had taken advantage of the limited educational prospects and schooled very hard, determined—unlike most of his school friends, who didn't fight against the inevitability of following in their fathers' footsteps—to escape the sleepy village and make a name for himself in the desert kingdom.

His good intentions had eventually become outright ambition and then slowly, imperceptibly, an obsession with power and respect. He had gradually ostracized himself, unwittingly at first, from his friends and family until, almost inevitably, his quest for advancement had taken him to Imperial schoolings. Here he had learnt about business, about tax and finance and law. He had learnt to be ruthless and analytical, to sacrifice reason for logic and to gain a lyrical understanding of the complex art of bureaucracy. He had severed the final ties to his roots in Gorner without hesitation when he'd been offered a place in the Imperial Academy, where he'd achieved with brains and cunning what most achieved with muscle and contacts—an officer rank in the Regulators.

He had been back to Gorner only once since then, where he'd been greeted with cold politeness, as a stranger in what had once been his home. The warm village life had left him feeling an outsider, bitterly cold and alienated. For a moment, he had wondered how long it had been since he had laughed, not the loud booming laugh he used when a superior cracked a joke, but genuinely laughed as his old friends and family seemed to do every day.

No matter, he had thought. *They're jealous of my success. Most of them will never leave this dead-end little village unless it is to sell corn on the market.*

As he'd impressed his way up the ranks of officer-hood with quite causal ease, it had only occurred to him just as he was surrendering to sleep at night that perhaps the villagers would all lead much happier lives than his, that perhaps contentment could come without success. These thoughts were dismissed by morning, when Muntave had continued to lash his silver tongue and drive his analytical brain until the day when, some years later, he'd been appointed sheriff of the very city he had fled from so many years ago.

Muntave enjoyed his position in Nastre. It was a peaceful and undemanding station, and his power over the king allowed him luxuries not always granted to a sheriff. But all of that seemed set to change. He knew it was likely, when his failure was made apparent, that he would be transferred to somewhere where life was not so easy. He shuddered as he thought of a posting in the tough frontier stations. The deep south lands of Barruk, where orcen tribes still randomly raided and terrorized. Or the far east postings, where elfen citizens protested almost continually against Imperial occupation.

Worse, he thought, was the possibility of being posted even further west, where Imperial forces still struggled to find a foothold in the strange, demon-infested lands of Dead Country. He briefly considered a life of struggle where monsters and species rarely seen these days in Regalious were still thriving. Prison would be better. Better than pitting sword and flintlock against giggling jeckles or cold-fleshed dedmen. That was a job for the young, strong, and foolish. Not for one accustomed to the flabby and bureaucratic lifestyle of a backwater sheriff.

He shivered again and jumped to his feet as Bentive, his personal assistant, came crashing into his quarters.

"Forgive me, sire—" Bentive began, breathing heavily as if having run a long way.

"What news?" interrupted Muntave, his manner cool and commanding despite the nervousness that knotted his intestines.

"The Argustin delegation has been spotted, sire."

Muntave looked out of his chamber window, a far-away melancholy taking over his features. "How long?" he said.

"Perhaps a few hours, sire."

"You may leave."

Bentive bowed and left the room. Muntave wondered if anyone would ever bow to him again after today.

The delegate had arrived sooner than he had expected. Presumably airboat technology had advanced since he had last been in the Empire's heart. It was likely. Muntave sighed and straightened his collar, preparing to meet his fate with as much dignity as he could muster.

———

BIP AND HANDEN rode out across the desert, their new companion holding on tightly behind Handen as he was jolted and jiggled by unaccustomed horsemanship. Their mounts panted in the crippling heat of the day. Handen was riding them harder than he would have recommended in other situations, traveling even through the lethal sunbeat of the afternoon. He suspected it would be necessary. Even though it was unlikely that their pursuers knew which direction they had set out in, and the constant desert winds would have obscured any of their tracks, Handen thought it only a matter of time until the Regulators started making educated assumptions about where the fugitives would be likely to pass through. After all, no one could survive out in the Bone Desert for long.

With this in mind, Handen's goal was to get out of the desert before the Empire had enough time to react to their escape and organize a manhunt. It was risky, especially with the adventurer's horse carrying two, but a small group traveling fast would always have a head start on a larger one, which would be more difficult to co-ordinate across hostile terrain. And, with any luck, it would be some time before their disappearance was discovered.

They rode almost continuously, stopping every couple of hours for a short rest for the sake of the horses before moving on again. They halted and made a cold camp only once during the night, taking the time to eat, savoring the dried meat and hot Nastren coffee and feeling their energy replenish. After a short nap, during which

Handen kept watch, they were on the move again, too fatigued even to talk to one another.

The possibility of riding the mounts into exhaustion before reaching a place of safety had occurred to Handen often, and once again, he found himself relying on an element of luck to ensure their survival. He grimaced into the sandy breeze of the Bone Desert, looking across at the drawn face of Bip and feeling the slacking grip of the dozing thief behind him.

They would try their luck.

MUNTAVE MOPPED his brow with a gray lace handkerchief. He was sweating far more than the heat of the day called for, especially since he was standing in the cool stone shade of the palace courtyard.

Nastre did not have an airdock and the courtyard, being the widest piece of uncluttered land in the city, would have to serve.

Muntave had already looked through the telescope at the arriving airboat, but he looked again, praying he was wrong. He wasn't. The narrow airboat (sleeker and better crafted than the civilian carriers, designed for speed rather than cargo carrying) was adorned with the colors not just of Argustin, but also of Dawncastle itself. Any hopes Muntave had harbored of the delegate being of similar rank to his own evaporated instantaneously. Dawncastle was the base of operations for the Emperor himself, and anyone sent directly from there would be a Pin Constable at least.

To his right, Bentive stood to rigid attention. Bentive, whose mannerisms and thin moustache reminded Muntave so much of himself when he had been a young man. Bentive, who would most likely climb up the ranks until he too was sheriff. Or perhaps even Grand Constable. Muntave took a moment to wonder whether Bentive was sacrificing as much as he had once sacrificed for his ambition.

He tried not to let his nervousness show as the airboat, now hovering overhead, was tethered to the palace walls. Eventually the guide rope for the balloon crane was lowered into the center of the courtyard. The quartet of musicians Muntave had hastily prepped for the arrival began a trumpet fanfare that lasted until the balloon-tethered elevator eventually touched down.

The assembled crowd waited as the balloon crane was tied, all eager to see who would emerge from the ornate passenger trunk. Two footmen abseiled quickly from the airboat above and opened the double doors. By some unseen device, a red carpet flicked gracefully out of the passenger compartment doorway and rolled across the courtyard. A dozen burly soldiers dressed in the black and silver colors of Dawncastle stamped out to form an honor guard along the edges of the carpet. The soldiers—each one's face obscured by a heavy, black helm—each clutched a hulking flintlock rifle, heavy enough fire power to bring down a jabberwocky should need be. Muntave's heart caught in his throat as a figure began to emerge from the balloon crane.

Emperor Tomberry Torrid Draegul the Tenth came forth into the daylight.

There was no mistaking him—most every citizen of Regalious knew the Emperor's likeness, be it from coin or statue, tapestry or commemorative plate. His face was pale, smooth, and delicate, near flawless but for the hooded cast of his eyes. With long, raven hair held back by the silver band of his crown, Draegul looked younger than his forty years. He verged on handsome, but something in the set of his gaze and the crook of his smile made his features unnerving.

He wore the silver and black robes of his station along with the symbolic katana at his hip and the rifle slung over his shoulder. These weapons, ornate and beautiful so as to represent the majesty and might of the Empire, were nonetheless kept primed and ready, each respectively sharpened and loaded every day.

He made an impressive figure, half mythic warrior and half bonny prince.

Though if you heard him laugh, or talked to him about his passions, doubtless your perceptions of him would change. The noble features would become the cold face of a killer. The regal stature would become the conspiring hunch of the chronic schemer.

Draegul looked like a hero. He thought like a villain. Too many people realized this too late.

Muntave had no trouble falling to his knees with the rest of the assemblage; in fact, he would have been very hard pressed to stand up. The musical quartet, who had faltered momentarily, began to play the Argustin anthem, and the Emperor walked along the carpet toward the sheriff. Muntave tried to control his visible quaking as the Emperor approached. He knelt down and kissed the ground in front of him, as was customary.

"You may rise," said Draegul. His voice was light but not melodious.

Muntave got slowly to his feet but remained looking at the floor. He fought hard to keep the stutter from his voice. "Your Holiness, this is a most pleasant surprise."

"Isn't it, though?" said Draegul. "I do like to get out and about now and again, you know. See how my Empire is flourishing." His voice hardened almost imperceptibly. "How my trusted lieutenants are fairing."

Muntave looked up and caught the cold gaze from the Emperor's deep black eyes. He had a sudden urge to throw himself to the floor and cry for forgiveness, and felt his knees struggling to comply.

"Where are the prisoners?" Draegul said casually, as though he had traveled several hundred miles just to make small talk.

Muntave's mouth flapped of its own accord for a while, desperately trying to form the correct words. Finally, they came. "They've escaped."

The Emperor continued to stare at the sheriff for what seemed like an eternity. "Blungkit?" he said eventually.

Muntave's gaze tore itself away from the Emperor's to the man who flanked his right shoulder like some dark conscience. He wore the neatly cut uniform of a Panthalus province Regulator, but he had the face of a street vagrant. His mouth gleamed wetly as he talked.

"Yes, Your Greatness?" he said.

"Shoot this man in the heart."

"Yes, Your Greatness."

Muntave's mouth only had time to form a quizzical "o" before Blungkit drew his flintlock and fired, blowing a neat, wide hole in the sheriff's chest. Muntave fell to his knees once more and looked up into the black eyes of the Emperor. They were cold and dismissive, but undoubtedly predatory, as though an animal madness lived behind the calm features of Bersch's most powerful man.

Like a shark, Muntave thought, and then he died.

The courtyard rang with silence, the assemblage trying desperately not to show how horrified they were. Bentive made a slight burping noise. Some of Muntave's blood had splashed on his tunic. To his horrified surprise, he realized the Emperor was pointing at him.

"You are now sheriff of Nastre," he said.

Bentive saluted smartly, then gestured to a couple of the stunned Nastren guards to dispose of the body of his predecessor. Despite his shock and disgust, he could not conceal a thin smile. Promotion came quickly when you worked close to the Emperor.

"Well, well, well!" said Draegul suddenly, an odd chirpiness making his flat voice sound almost pleasant. "This is a turn-up for the books, isn't it, Blungkit?"

Blungkit still stood smartly to his Emperor's right, his smoking pistola safely holstered again. "Yes, sire," he said indifferently.

"It seems the doomsayers have eluded you again," said Draegul. There was an accusatory undertone to his pleasantness and he made no show of hiding it.

Blungkit's face remained impassive. Since reporting the escape of the two fugitives, Blungkit had been more than surprised when the Emperor had taken a personal interest in the investigation. When Draegul had learned that the wooden-toothed Regulator was partly responsible for the escape, he had, much to everyone's surprise, promoted the him to Pin Constable—a position surpassing the rank of general in the Imperial army—and subsequently made him personally responsible for the recapture of the fugitives. Blungkit, whose thoughts were large and blundering things, had nonetheless realized that his promotion was also his punishment—should he fail in his duties, his life would more than likely be forfeit. Muntave's sudden and violent death was testament to that.

"They shan't elude me for long, sire," he said.

"Really?" said Draegul. "What makes you so sure? They've made a very good job of it so far."

Blungkit was not classically educated. Nor was he trained from birth for higher thinking. Certainly the bloodline of a thousand Emperors did not flow through his veins. He was a man who had cut his teeth on hard streets and had earned a diploma in treading on people's necks. However, he was beginning to realize that the Emperor was a man after his own heart. He knew a nasty, vindictive bastard when he saw one, and Draegul was one of the best. Blungkit respected that.

"They would have gone into the desert, sire. No question. They'll be expecting us to follow them in, no doubt, and be inconvenienced by the terrain."

The Emperor smiled. One of the many talents he prided himself on was his judgement of character, and he had certainly been proved right in his assessment of Blungkit. The man was just stubborn enough to take the escape of the doomsayers personally, and by far nasty enough to hunt them to the ends of Bersch if needed. Draegul knew that Blungkit, even without the threat of death hanging over his head, would dog the fugitives relentlessly and rabidly.

"What is your plan, then, Pin Constable?"

"Easy one, sire. Just a process of deduction, if you like." Blungkit began to count down on his meaty fingers. "Everyone's on high alert back in the city provinces, so we don't have to worry about them going north. They wouldn't last more than a week in the Bone Desert, so we can forget about them going west. Same for south. So that only leaves east to worry about, the Dozantyne Shrub."

Draegul smiled. Blungkit was a useful man. Like all good policemen, he had the mind of a criminal.

Blungkit continued. "I suggest we skirt around the desert to the telegraph station, organize reinforcements, and head south 'til we cuts through their trail."

"Excellent!" Draegul clapped his delicate hands. "You're a god-ugly baboon's rump of a man, Blungkit, but you make a damn good Pin Constable. Keep this up, and I might think twice about having you flayed alive."

Despite the joviality of Draegul's tone, Blungkit knew he was being deadly serious. "Thank you, sire," he said.

"And now I'm afraid I must leave you. I have other matters to attend to."

"As you will, sire," said Blungkit. He waited until the Emperor boarded the balloon crane before turning back to the shell-shocked Nastren Guard.

"All right, you useless shower of bastards, let's move!"

$$7$$

The Dozantyne Shrub

There was a garden. It was lovely. That was the only word he could think of, really. It was peaceful, certainly, well kept, definitely. But the word that kept coming back to him was "lovely."

He looked down at the cup and saucer in his hands, and though the day was pleasantly warm, he appreciated the hot ceramic in his hand. A sweet smell rose up from the cup. He couldn't place it, but the smell was relaxing.

He felt totally at peace. He tried to think of the last time he'd felt this relaxed but couldn't. Other times and places seemed a little fuzzy in the garden.

There was another man there. He sat across from him in a deck chair, sipping something from his own cup. He seemed pleasant enough, with his broad face and his wiry gray hair held down by a well-worn flat cap. He appeared to be the gardener.

"It's lovely," said Bip.

The man turned to him as if acknowledging him for the first time.

"The garden," said Bip, dreamily. "It's lovely. "

"Thank you," said the man. "I try to keep it neat. "

Bip seemed to wake up a bit. He couldn't remember how he had got there. "Who are you?" he said.

The man slurped noisily from his cup. "I'm Ted," he said. "Pleased to meet you."

"What is this place?" said Bip.

"This is my garden," said Ted. He wasn't patronizing, but there was an amused twinkle in his eye.

"It's lovely," said Bip again. He couldn't think what else to say. "You must spend a lot of time on it."

Ted nodded sagely, his flat cap bobbing up and down on his head. "All the time in the world," he said.

A sudden surreal feeling swept over Bip. It felt a little like when Mr. Random visited, but without the nagging incongruity.

"Who are you really?" asked Bip.

"I told you," Ted replied. "I'm Ted."

"Then what are you?"

The older man laughed, and there was something about that laugh that made Bip feel totally at ease. "A better question! Much better. But do you really want the answer?"

Bip looked at the old man. He felt sleepy, suddenly, as if having just woken from a pleasant dream. He nodded his head.

"I'm commonly known as the Universal Theory. Though Ultra-versal Theory might be more accurate. Or, if you liked, you could call me the Creation Equation, the Infinite Balance, The Master Plan, or the Only Blueprint. Though Ted will suffice, for now."

Bip nodded. Despite the vastness of what he had just been told, he didn't feel at all surprised. He felt quite calm, actually.

"I expect you'd probably like me to elaborate?" prompted Ted.

Bip nodded again. There seemed little else he could do.

"To put it in layman's terms, imagine if everything in the universes is the answer to a long and drawn out question. Well, I'm that question."

Bip nodded. "God?" he said.

Ted laughed a little. "No, no," he said. "Quite different." He paused to sip more of his tea before continuing. "I am the thing that unites all energies within the spectrum of existence, the hand that weaves the strings. Across the length of all dimensions, I am the common denominator. I'm a sort of a metaphysical embodiment of the nature of the Ultraverse. If infinity is a story, then I am the one reading it aloud, for no story can exist without a reader." Ted put down his cup and looked Bip straight in the eye. "Because of me: Everything."

Bip looked blank for a while. "Everything is a gardener?" he ventured.

Ted laughed again. "This?" he said, gesturing around him. "This is just window dressing. A place I like to bring people. A face I like to show."

"What are you like really?" said Bip.

"I could show you the bright lights of hidden galaxies. I could take you to voids verging on infinity. I could show you the tiniest daisy in a field, because all of these things are me. I am the Soul of the Whole. I am the question of which all other questions were born."

Bip leaned back in his deckchair. "That's nice," he said.

They drank tea in silence. Bip was surprised by the smooth sweetness of the concoction. *Like back in Kaneq,* he thought. *Milk, two sugars.*

"I suppose your next question will be 'why?'" said Ted after a while.

"Why what?" Bip replied dreamily.

"Why are you here?"

"I don't know!"

"Exactly!"

They looked at each other for a while. Ted waited for Bip to catch up. The garden could be distracting, he knew.

"I wanted to let you know a little about what you're up against," said Ted. "In this universe, everything is going as the plan intended. But there are those who would go against the plan."

"The Discordance," said Bip.

"Not just the Discordance," said Ted. "Every conscious being has the ability to challenge the blueprint."

"What happens when they do?" Bip interrupted.

"What happens when an unstoppable force meets an immovable object?" replied Ted.

"There's a massive explosion?" ventured Bip.

"No."

"A massive implosion?"

"No. The unstoppable force stops, the immovable object moves." Ted leaned back in his deckchair.

Bip looked blank.

"Nothing is infallible," said Ted. "Not even me. If the blueprint of a universe is changed, then the blueprint is changed. But this is not always for the better and more often than not is for the worse. That is why there are those who would actively prevent interference to appropriate causality."

"The Clarions?"

"Amongst many, yes. The Caretakers, as I believe they are known in this neck of the Ultraverse."

"You needn't worry about me," said Bip, suddenly worried about why he was being told all this. "I'm with the good guys. Order over chaos. Yep, that's me!"

Ted looked at the Kaneqian long and hard. "I know you are a good man, Bip—I can see these things—but you must realize that what you think of as order and chaos are not necessarily good or bad."

"What do you mean?" said Bip.

Ted clucked his tongue and looked thoughtful for a moment.

Suddenly a bright light flashed, and Bip found himself in a long, well-lit room.

The lights here reminded him of the ones back in the Dome. Before him was what appeared to be a huge picture, though picture was a lenient word. It looked mostly like a humungous wash of unplanned color. Bip started as Ted appeared beside him.

"Where are we?" asked Bip.

"In the Tate Modern. An art gallery in a place called London in a galaxy and universe not too dissimilar to your own."

"Why are we here?" said Bip, glancing around the deserted hall. He could see other artworks now. All neatly displayed behind fuzzy rope of some kind.

"To look at the paintings, of course." Ted grinned. "I wanted to show you this one in particular."

Bip looked at the colossal typhoon of paint before him. "I don't see what's so special about it," he said.

"Come away with me a bit," said Ted. He placed his hand on Bip's shoulder, and the Kaneqian wobbled uneasily as he felt himself being carried back along the corridor without the movement of his legs being involved. To his surprise, the indecipherable mess of the painting slowly transformed into a picture of an attractive woman. Bip gasped at the optical illusion.

"You see?" said Ted. "Where there first appears to be only chaos, there is order. A planned design."

"Wow," breathed Bip.

"But that's not the point I'm trying to make," said Ted, and waved his hand. There was another bright light and then before him the painting still hung, but against a backdrop of stars and blackness. Bip looked around and clung terrified to Ted's shoulder as he realized he was standing on an infinite star-studded void.

"It's okay, Bip," said Ted, and Bip calmed. Something about Ted's voice was instantly soothing. "Now see here," said the gardener, and pointed at the painting that now hung eerily in the void. Then all of a sudden, Bip felt himself being moved backward again, this time countless miles rather than the length of a museum corridor. As his perspective widened, he saw not just one picture but dozens, then hundreds, then uncountable millions. Soon he was looking at one gargantuan picture, the same unplanned mess he had first seen in the museum.

"And order gives way to chaos," said Ted. "But wait, there's more."

Bip felt the sensation of being drawn back again. The huge mess of a picture gave way to the picture of the woman once again, hanging in the stars like some ancient goddess. This time, though, they did not stop to regard the picture, but continued to draw back. The picture once again gave way to thousands, which once again gave way to the chaotic mess, which once again became the woman. This happened again and again until Bip thought he was going to be sick.

"Order, chaos; chaos, order," said Ted in a singsong-ish voice.

"Stop," said Bip, weakly. "Stop, please."

The bright light flashed once more, and once again they were in the garden. Bip felt instantly at peace.

"You see?" said Ted. "Chaos and Order. Order and Chaos. Really just two ways of looking at the same thing."

Bip nodded. It made sense. He thought of the shapes you could find in clouds sometimes, if you looked the right way. Though it might just be your imagination, it didn't necessarily mean the patterns weren't there.

"The Discordance believe that chaos is the natural state of the universe and, therefore, chaos must be created via the destruction of order. The Clarions believe that the natural state of the universe is order and that order must be protected and maintained." Ted refilled his cup from the teapot. "So you see, both are a little wrong, both are a little right. What they don't seem to acknowledge is what I have just shown you—that order and chaos both have their places in the ultra-verse—are, indeed, both one and the same depending on where you're standing."

Bip thought about what had been said for a while. "What are you getting at?" he asked finally.

"That the only trouble with either belief comes when the universal plan is challenged by the assertion of those beliefs."

Bip nodded, keeping up.

"Now," continued Ted, "I'll warrant you, it's usually the Discordance that are the troublemakers. Most of the Caretakers leave things well enough alone unless there's interference—which is fine. But this time. This time things are different."

A slow and horrible understanding was beginning to creep up on Bip. "What do you mean?"

Ted sighed wearily. "The destruction of Bersch is part of this universe's plans, part of its blueprint. It has nothing to do with the Discordance."

Bip's jaw fell nearly to his chest. "But that's impossible," he flustered. "Handen said… Mr. Random even said!"

Ted held up a hand almost apologetically. "I know what you've been told, but the Caretakers made a mistake. The interference they detected was from another incident. The Massive Ball of Death heading for Bersch is my doing—it's all part of the blueprint."

"You can't do that!" said Bip. Suddenly the garden didn't seem very serene anymore.

"Can't I?" said Ted, raising his bushy eyebrows. "I already told you; I'm not a God. Not a Greatdevil, neither. I am just what is."

"What are you asking of me?" cried Bip. "To sit back and watch as a planet explodes? The one I'm standing on?"

"What I am telling you, Bip, is that the Massive Ball of Death is not the work of the Discordance."

"No! I know that! It's your bloody work, isn't it? You're the one responsible. Why are you even telling me this?"

Ted sipped his tea casually. "I am the Infinite Balance. I like to make sure everything's fair, to a degree. I thought it fair you should know that the Discordance are not responsible for the astral disaster that will destroy Bersch."

Bip frowned. He could hear what Ted was saying, but he seemed to be hinting at something else. Bip wished he could work out what but was too confused and frightened to think straight. A sudden and terrible thought occurred to Bip.

"Why didn't the distress call the *Sentinel* sent ever reach the Clarions? Or any other of the Caretakers? Why was no help sent? Was that because of the Discordance or because of you?"

Ted sighed again. "The lightwave was intercepted by a deep-space project of a much more primitive civilization. They spent a good three hundred years trying to decipher it before they filed it away for good."

"So, in other words, it was you?"

"It was part of the blueprint, yes." Ted patted Bip on the knee. "You can't take the universe personally, you know."

"I can bloody well try!" huffed Bip. "You can't expect me to sit back and watch the world explode! You said that anyone could challenge the plan—well that's just what I'm going to do!"

"That's your prerogative as a conscious being," said Ted. "I'd advise against it, though."

"Yeah, well…" said Bip, and couldn't think of any intelligent retort. "Bollocks to you!" he finished lamely. "Send me back, right now! I want to go!"

Ted smiled sadly. "As you wish," he said, and there was a bright light.

After Bip was gone, Ted got to his feet and went back to tending his garden. "He'll go far, that one," he muttered to himself.

BIP OPENED his eyes to see the ground rushing past his face. He heard the jingle and clop of horses, and, when a stirrup flew into his field of vision, he realized he must be hanging over his saddle. His head pounded, and a taste of vomit burned his mouth slightly. He felt as though somebody had hung him out to dry.

"Urrk?" he managed, and the sound of the horses changed. The ground stopped moving beneath him, and he was pulled from his saddle and lowered onto the ground. Above him, the concerned seriousness of Handen's face and the conspiring smirk of Azron's came into view against the painfully bright sky.

"All right, mate?" said Azron. "Have a nice kip, did we?"

"What happened?" managed Bip.

"You fainted," said Handen. "Sunstroke."

"How long was I out?" murmured Bip.

"The best part of a day. Sorry for the discomfort, but we couldn't risk stopping and waiting for you to wake up."

Bip thought back to his time in the garden. Even now it was beginning to feel like a dream. Except that some part of him knew it wasn't. As bizarre as the experience had been, something within Bip insisted it was probably the most real thing that had ever happened to him.

"You were talking in your sleep, mate," said Azron. "Having a right old prattle, you were."

"Something about a garden?" Handen prompted.

"I can't remember," lied Bip. Whatever his experience with Ted had meant for his future, he meant to deal with it by himself. He doubted whether he would ever tell Handen or Azron about it. After all, with each second that passed, Ted and the garden seemed more and more like a fever-dream.

It wasn't, though, whispered a solemn part of Bip's subconscious; *it was as real as the nose on your face. Maybe more so.*

"Where are we?" he said, changing the subject. His throat felt raw and sandy.

"Actually, you woke up just in time," said Handen. "We left the last of the Bone Desert behind us a few hours ago. And as luck would have it, there seems to be a settlement a few miles away."

"Running a bit low on water," said Azron by way of explanation. "Not to mention horse power."

Now that Bip concentrated, he could hear the heavy wheezing of their mounts. They had come close to running them into exhaustion, and they needed rest badly if they were to carry on. He didn't blame them; he wasn't feeling too good himself. His head felt baked from the sunstroke and he found himself wishing once more that he hadn't exploded his traveling hat.

With the help of his two companions, Bip rose unsteadily to his feet. He waited until his head stopped spinning before he focused on the far-away settlement. When he could finally see well enough to make sense of the blurred buildings, a smile broke over his face.

"It looks like a ranch," he said.

"Yep," said Handen. "And ranches mean horses. With any luck, we won't have to stop for longer than it takes to trade in for some new mounts. Maybe even a wagon."

With some effort, Bip managed to clamber back onto his horse. He waited a while until the dizziness in his head passed, then rode toward the ranch.

———

THE DOZANTYNE SHRUB was a relief from the harsh desolation of the Bone Desert, though not by much. Compared to most of the lands of Regalious, which tended to be prairie or hillside, Dozantyne was a wilderness of hardpan soil and low, flat horizons. The ground was cracked and wrinkled, the face of a hallowed ancient, its beard a fine furze of the shriveled dry weeds that were the Shrub's namesake. Though there was life here, it kept itself hunkered down in the drawling siesta of the Dozantyne afternoons, waiting for the evenings when life would become suddenly quick and aggressive.

Far off in the drowsy air, a vulture cried. No one would comfort it.

There were canyons in the Shrub, deep pits and crevices where the shade inspired tiny, thriving sub-ecologies. There were mountains of a sort, too, though they were really nothing more than giant boulders standing lonely and ridiculous in the squat surroundings. There were even forests: great clusters of long-dead trees standing dry and brittle like corpses, a tombstone reminder of the millennia ago when the Shrub had perhaps been more hospitable. In these zombie woods, deep-down creatures would bide, waiting for the stupid and the curious...

For now, though, the Shrub was merely flat and featureless, lazy geography under a tired sky. The sun always kept a watchful eye over the southlands, so the heat was still intense, though not as raging as the desert left behind them.

Amidst this slightly dreamy hell, it was quite odd to see the merry little patch of life that was the ranch. Though its stables and fencing had a distinctly home-made look about them, they were newly painted and well maintained—odd totems of freshness in this ageing landscape.

From the flat-roofed farmhouse, a man emerged. He wore a ten-gallon hat, although set above his short frame, it looked more like a twenty-gallon. The man stepped into the dusty day and grinned with benevolent optimism, his dark glasses reflecting the hostile glare of the sun and his bushy white beard shining brilliantly in the daylight. He surveyed the horizon and noted, with some pride, the complete lack of incident. Something caught his eye, however, and caused him to furrow his tangled brows. There were riders in the distance. Coming his way. In a sudden burst of movement, the man sprinted into back into his house and quickly re-emerged with what looked like a couple of boards. He sprinted to the gateways of the ranch and hooked the wooden boards onto it. Together they formed a sign that read, "Bolan Ranch—Information and Bookings." The man waited beneath the sign with a wide and welcoming grin slicing through his beard.

———

WHEN BIP first approached the ranch, he felt pretty sure he'd lost his mind. He read the sign in its large gaudy lettering and thought, briefly, that the months of hard riding were finally taking their toll on him. His opinion was reinforced when he rode close enough to see the neon smile of the man beneath the sign, whose huge hat jarred against his loudly colored shirt. Before Bip could frame a question, the man was speaking in familiarly eager tones.

"Howdy! Howdy! Howdy! Howdy and Yee-haw! Welcome to Bolan Ranch—the most secluded, luxurious ranch getaway in the whole of the Wild Souths!"

Handen and Azron exchanged puzzled glances. Bip continued to stare open-mouthed at the familiar face before him.

"Yep!" the old man continued. "If it's the serenity of the open plains you're after, then you're in the right place! Bolan Ranch is the perfect holiday from the hustle and bustle of city life!"

"Excuse me," began Bip.

"While you're here why not try…"

"Pardon me."

"…tumbleweed surprise?! Mmm mmm! Surprisingly weedy!"

"*Hey!*"

The old man stopped, looking first confused, then a little miffed at having his sales pitch interrupted. "Yeah?" he said.

"Bolan?" Bip said.

"Bing! Two points!" replied Bolan, pumping his fist with annoying enthusiasm. Bip blinked owlishly for a while.

"How did you get here so fast?"

Bolan looked around, the grin on his face becoming uneasy. "Don't know what you mean, partner, I've been here all day."

"But you were on the island," said Bip. "Bolan Cay?"

Bolan looked over his dark glasses skeptically. "You must mean that no-good brother of mine. Island holiday resort, right?"

"Yes, that's right," said Bip, though he thought the term "holiday resort" a bit generous.

"Pah! Waste of time," said Bolan, disdainfully. "I told him from the start that no one wants to go all the way to his stupid little island for a holiday—not when they've got God's country right on their doorsteps!" Bolan opened his arms expansively, taking in the half-dead landscape of the Shrub. Bip looked around. If this was God's country, then he'd happily holiday in hell, given a choice.

Bolan's expression became suddenly worried. He leaned forward conspiringly. "He didn't have no customers, did he?" he said.

"Well...no," replied Bip.

"Hah!" Bolan grinned hugely. "I told him! I told him all along! Bolan Cay? Hah! No one wants to go to a stupid island!"

Bip frowned at the deserted ranch. "It doesn't exactly seem to be the busy season for you either," he pointed out.

"Yeah, well," said Bolan, reproachfully. "The ranch is having teething problems, that's all. Once the word gets around about this place, the tourists will stampede, I tells ya!"

Yeah, thought Bip, *stampede all the way to somewhere else.*

"Now, what can I do you boys for?" said Bolan, rubbing his hands together. Handen, who had been watching this exchange with a mixture of puzzlement and impatience, decided it was time to get to the point. "We need fresh horses," he said.

Bolan waved his hands dismissively. "Can't you read the sign? I'm no goldarn merchant! I only got a couple of horses and a wagon, and they're for my Scenic Wilderness Tours!"

Azron put a hand over his face. There was a sound that could have been a cough but was more likely muffled laughter.

"They sound fine," said Handen, coolly. "We'll take them."

"Now you listen here, mister! Thems horses are part of my livelihood, and I won't sells them for nothing or nobody!" Bolan crossed his arms stubbornly.

There was a dull clunk as a lump of gold landed in the dust by the old man's feet. It was quite a large lump. Bolan gasped. His passion might have been the ranch, but at his heart, he was a businessman. That lump of gold could buy a hell of a lot of scenic wilderness tours.

Bolan looked up and grinned his huge, white grin. "I tell you what, boys, you got yourselves a deal!"

A FEW HOURS LATER, Bolan watched as the three strangers left the ranch riding a horse-drawn wagon with the legend "Bolan Ranch Scenic Wilderness Tours" painted on its side in huge, bouncy letters. They had stopped only long enough to refill their waterskins and load up the wagon, taking advantage of some of the supplies Bolan had thrown in as part of the deal. With his newly acquired lump of gold, the possibilities for Bolan seemed endless.

Maybe I can finally build those extra guest rooms, thought Bolan, *for when business picks up.*

He watched the trio ride off into the uneventful sunset and felt a rise of gratitude.

"Y'all come back now, ya hear?" he called.

BIP LEANED BACK in the seat of the covered wagon, relaxing as the fresh horses pulled them on at a steady pace, spurred on by Handen at the reins. He felt better now he had been rested and watered. The sun was being kept from his head by a souvenir sombrero Bolan had given him. It was a nice hat, though unfortunately had "I love Bolan Ranch" written across its brim.

Azron was stretched out in the back of the wagon, smoking a cigarette and blowing smoke rings, which lingered in the air while the wagon pulled away.

"I don't see why we had to give him all that gold," he said.

"How else were we supposed to buy the horses?" said Handen.

"I could've just nicked 'em," grumbled Azron. "Wouldn't have taken long." Handen sighed. "I remind you we've got half of the Empire after us. The Emperor himself even seems to have taken a personal interest in our capture. An old man with a pocket full of gold is less likely to tell tales than an old man whose horses have just been stolen."

"Fair enough," said Azron. "But it still seemed like a lot of gold to just throw on the floor like that."

Bip looked at Handen. He'd had similar thoughts himself and wondered how much, if any, of the gold was left. He marveled briefly at how what had been a lump of relatively worthless metal in Kaneq had suddenly become so important to him.

"We'll be okay," said Handen. "I don't think we'll have much opportunity to spend it for a while, anyway."

The wagon rolled across the Shrub, kicking up dust as it went. Azron looked at a small wooden doll with a cowboy hat and a flowery shirt. He had, of course, filled his pockets up at Bolan Ranch, mostly with useless souvenirs and trinkets—not anything of worth. It was the principle that counted. He was, after all, a thief.

THEY STOPPED THAT NIGHT, more for the benefit of the horses than the passengers, who had taken turns steering in shifts, giving the opportunity for rest throughout the long day. They set up camp after the sun set. The wide-open expanses of the Shrub glowed pleasantly in the starlight, and the trio was able to set up camp unhindered by the darkness. A small fire was lit, more for the look of the thing than the necessity; unlike the Bone Desert, the nights in the Dozantyne Shrub were quite warm. There was no wind, and the heat of the day radiated from the baked earth beneath them.

The three sat around the fire while Bip slowly cooked some of the fresh meat they had packed at Bolan's. Handen, using some of the utensils they'd picked up in Nastre, was boiling up some of the rich, sticky coffee. The smells combined in a tantalizing aroma, and Bip felt his stomach rumble in anticipation.

"So, then," said Azron. "I forgot to ask in all the commotion—how's the saving the world going?" There was a slight smirk on the thief's face that indicated he was still not quite convinced of Bip's story.

"Well, I took your advice," said Bip. "I tried warning the people in the smaller cities and towns first."

"Yeah? How did that go, then?" Azron said.

"They locked me in a lunatic asylum," said Bip, coldly.

"Oh."

There was a long pause that Handen took advantage of to pass around the tin mugs of Nastren coffee. Bip took his gratefully and slurped the hot beverage. He was beginning to take a liking to the bitter brew, but still missed the presence of milk and two sugars.

"Anyway," he said. "It wasn't all bad. I met Handen there, and it turns out that he's from Kaneq, too."

Azron raised a critical eyebrow. "Really? And you took his word for it, did you? What with him being in a nut house and all?"

"Well, you see, that's what I thought at first too, but it turned out he knew all sorts of things about Kaneq that no one could possibly know, and then it turns out, well, you remember I told you about the volunteers?"

Azron nodded.

"Well, Handen was the first!"

The thief paused mid-sip, the tin cup settled on his lip. "The first volunteer?" he said. His voice was thick and deliberate, as if talking to a slow child.

"That's right!" said Bip.

"The first volunteer who left hundreds of years ago?"

"Yep."

Azron looked from Bip to Handen and back again. Finally, he smiled broadly at Handen. "Well, I have to tell you, you're looking very good for your age."

Handen rolled his eyes. "I'm immortal," he said.

"Of course you are," said Azron. "You're an immortal, the world's going to end, and your friend here can explode things with his mind. Yeah, it all makes perfect sense, mate—perfect sense."

Handen gave a heavy sigh, and then, before Azron could react, he flipped a dagger from the sleeve of his leather coat and stabbed himself in the heart with it. A spray of blood doused half of the camp-fire with a reptilian hiss.

"Great holy bastards!" shouted Azron.

As the fire slowly regained its former luminescence, Azron was surprised to see Handen still sitting cross-legged, his face a mask of cool impatience. He had unbuttoned his shirt to reveal a dagger wound that closed up before the thief's astonished eyes.

The thief's normal countenance of the slightly amused indifference that passed for streetwise in Port Town had given way to a child-like expression of awe. He was quick to regain his composure, though.

"...magic," he breathed.

"Maybe," conceded Handen, and proceeded to tell Azron of the hidden fountain he had found in Ghulbra forest so many years ago, and while telling him, also filled in some of the gaps Bip had left about the off-worlders who had founded Kaneq in the first place. They ate the roasted meat, and the thief listened intently until the adventurer's story came to a finish.

"So, you see," said Handen. "It might just be magic, but all that means is that there's a scientific explanation I haven't found yet. I couldn't tell you without an in-depth bioscan."

"A what now?" muttered Azron.

"Well, it could be that the fountain of youth contained a parasitic microorganism that maintains and repairs the host that sustains it. Or it could be that the fountain held some sort of DNA code that unlocks a regeneration factor already present in humanoid life forms."

Azron blinked. "Or it could have just been magic..."

"Yeah," said Handen, wryly. "Either way, I'm stuck with it 'til I find the fountain of death."

"It all seems a bit far-fetched, though," said Azron.

"Yeah, well. That's life," said Handen, and shrugged nonchalantly before taking a long swig from his cooling coffee.

"Still," Azron said thoughtfully. "Being immortal; that must be pretty handy."

Handen's eyes went cold. "Can you imagine getting tired of stealing?" he said. Azron looked surprised. He was passionate about thievery. Thievery defined him. He was one of the best, and it had never occurred to him to ever give it up. He wasn't sure he could if he tried. As for getting tired of it… Well…maybe one day he'd retire, but he fondly suspected that, even as an old, old man, he would be stealing the pocket money from his grandchildren.

"Because that's what happens," Handen continued. "You get tired of everything."

The trio sat in silence for a while. Bip always felt a little uncomfortable when Handen brooded like this. When his mind was on the job, the former Hostilities Advisor's manner was quick and professional, but when things calmed down, he would become melancholic and withdrawn.

"Besides," said Handen, after a while, "I don't think the humanoid mind was meant to cope with such extended life spans. For a while when I was imprisoned, I became convinced that my former life was a madman's dream. I don't think it was just the Bin that did it to me. Even now most of my past, that which I can remember, seems unreal, as if it didn't actually happen. And a man without a past is no man at all."

The former Hostilities Advisor stared hard into the fire, and Bip wondered what ghosts and faces he saw in those flames.

"At least you have friends," said Azron, his half-ironic chirpiness returning to his voice. "My dad always said, 'As long as you've got mates, son, and a family that loves you, then you'll always have someone to bust you out of prison.'"

The three laughed. "Your dad seems like he was a very wise man," said Handen.

"Taught me everything I know," said Azron proudly. "They called him Billy the Lint, because of the amount of time he spent in people's pockets."

Bip laughed again, glad that the somber air of the camp had been cleared. Even Handen, who rarely smiled, couldn't keep the broad grin from lighting up his usually dark face.

"Come on," Handen said. "Let's get some sleep. We've a long ride ahead of us."

The three of them bunkered down under the wagon, appreciating the heat trapped there as the night began to cool around them.

As he drifted off to sleep, Azron thought about his new companions.

Saving the world, he thought, and smiled to himself, amused by the thought of the unknown number of law enforcers pursuing them. He was looking forward to playing at being a hero. It wasn't far off what he was used to as a thief.

THE MASSIVE BALL of Death careened through star system after star system, leaving a wake of radioactive dust and confusion in its path. It had accelerated, due to the favorable gravitational pulls of various planets, to near-incomprehensible speeds. It was getting to the stage where it was smashing through obstacles before it even realized there were obstacles to smash through. It didn't mind, though. The fledgling optimism of the nuclear cluster had grown to a frenzied anticipation. Nothing would stand in its way.

In the gamma sector of Beleris Six, a traffic patrol car floated in the gas giant and Romanis bypass. The distance between the two planets at certain points in their orbit was quite small, so the pass-between traffic was heavily policed lest some dangerous driver be sucked into the gravitational pull of either astral body.

Officer Lenny Lepowski sat in his patrol car, appreciating, as he had done for many years, the swirling magnitude of the gas giant through his monitors. Sometimes he would find the smoldering reds and oranges of the planet hypnotic and could stare for hours if uninterrupted.

Currently Lepowski was enjoying coffee and donuts. Lenny was an old, old officer and had seen much technological advancement in his lifetime. Heck, space-worthy patrol cars had only just been prototyped when he had joined the force those many, many years ago. He had seen advancements in medicine and science that had made him proud to be a Belerian. Coffee and donuts, though, were beyond improvement. Coffee and donuts had achieved the nexus of perfection centuries ago.

He had come to realize that they were an important part of being a police officer. Perhaps one of the most important parts of being a police officer. Without them, he thought, life just wouldn't seem complete. It just wouldn't feel right.

As a younger man, he had been interested in interstellar geography and history. He had been shocked and appalled to learn there were civilizations where donuts—and sometimes even coffee—had not yet been invented. There were civilizations where the policemen sat on horseback munching thoughtfully on pita bread and sipping herbal teas. It wasn't right. He knew that, deep down, these law enforcers of other worlds were missing something. They might not know what it was, but he knew they must lie awake at night sometimes, wondering what it was that was missing from their lives.

He pitied them. Then he ate another donut.

Suddenly his scanners began to beep manically. He sat bolt upright with a start and spilt some of his hot coffee down his shirt. He wasn't angry; he knew that spilling hot coffee in a comic fashion when you were disturbed suddenly was also an unshakable part of being a police officer.

His expression turned from irritation to surprise as the speeding object zoomed past his display monitors. It was impossible to gain a composition analysis, and the speed reading was too high for the computer to calculate right away. Lepowski felt the massive rumbling as the object passed, even though it was miles away from the bypass and his patrol car.

His gaze shifted nervously from monitor to monitor until the rumbling finally stopped. Then he ate another donut, chewing thoughtfully and holding his coffee with shaking hands.

He thought briefly about calling in the sighting and setting off in hot pursuit. Then he decided against it. After all, he only had two weeks 'til retirement.

The Massive Ball of Death moved on obliviously. Nothing would stand its way.

BOLAN SAT in the rocking chair on his porch, looking over his sleepy ranch at the flawless horizon beyond. *God's country,* he thought to himself, and lay back, smiling in the hot sunshine. *If you want peace and quiet, then this is the place to come. Yep! More peace and quiet than a sane man can handle.*

Bolan was disturbed from his reveries by a distant sound of thunder. He looked into the cloudless sky and frowned. Then, just on the edge of vision, he saw the dust trail rise into the sky. It was a few minutes before he could make out what was approaching, and his face dropped in dismay as an uneasy suspicion rose in his belly.

It's them! he thought. *It's the stampeding tourists! They've found me!*

A mixture of emotions flooded Bolan's body. He realized with sudden clarity that he didn't want a lot of customers after all. Just the odd couple now and then would have been fine, just enough that he could survive out in his ranch without being bothered. He mourned regretfully for his treasured peace and quiet.

A few minutes later, he realized that he had been wrong. The riders didn't look like tourists at all. They all wore uniforms for one thing, and Bolan doubted that tourists made a habit of traveling with uberbeasts. The rider at the head of the group rode over to Bolan. He dimly recognized the gray coat of the Regulators, and his thoughts turned sadly to the nice boys who had ridden through a couple of days ago. The nice boys he had sold a wagon to.

"Evening, old-timer," said the Regulator, touching the brim of his gray top hat. "Pin Constable Blungkit, at your service."

Bolan looked into the leering eyes of the newcomer and doubted very much that he was at anyone's service but his own. "I don't want no trouble, mister," he said, trying to keep the shake from his voice.

Blungkit grinned, his rank wooden teeth gleaming wetly in the sunshine. Having caught up to the doomsayer's trail so quickly, he was in a good mood, so suppressed the urge to boot the old man in the face. "And you won't have any, either. As long as you feel you can answer a few simple questions," he said.

Bolan didn't say anything.

"Now," said Blungkit, with a merry tone in his voice, "I know for a fact that a couple of guys rode through here quite recently. Maybe even three of them. They would have been in a hurry."

Bolan was thankful he was still wearing his dark glasses. He didn't want to look this Regulator in the eye.

"Maybe you seen them," continued Blungkit. "Maybe you even helped them."

Bolan looked at the ground. He was as scared as he had ever been in his isolated old age.

"Yeah, you probably did. Nice old-timer like you. Probably bent over backward for the buggers. See, I'd be willing to overlook that, I would. If you was willing to help me out a little..."

Bolan looked up. He thought briefly about defying this man. After all, what could he do? Then he gazed into Blungkit's eyes. The cold eyes of a drunken snake. This man could do a lot if he wanted to. And he would enjoy doing it, as well. Bolan had never felt so hungry for the peace and quiet he had become accustomed to.

"And I wouldn't think about lying to me, neither," Blungkit added. "'Cause I will catch up to those whoresons, and I will find out if you helped them. Aiding and abetting that is," he hissed. "A punishable offence."

The Regulator waited for this to sink in. Bolan looked at the ground again.

"Now," said Blungkit, "you tell me which direction they went in, or I'm going to start setting fire to things."

Wordlessly, Bolan pointed in the direction the boys had traveled in, feeling a wash of relief and shame as he did so.

"Thank you very much, squire," said Blungkit, and spat unthinkingly on the ground, hawking monstrously as he did. "You're a good citizen."

The Regulator rode off to join his troops and began riding east, as Bolan had indicated.

The old man felt terrible, but more than that he felt relieved as the dust cloud disappeared over the horizon, and peace and quiet returned to his ranch once more. He sat back in his rocking chair again and shivered. Where ever Blungkit had come from, he didn't belong in God's country.

Boredom, Bedlam, and Birdmen

Bip lazed in the back of the wagon, enjoying the relief from the heat of the day. Azron had reluctantly taken the reins, and it was Bip's turn to lie down.

They had been traveling through the Shrub for a just over a week now and were moving along at a very satisfactory pace. They had fallen into the routine of each man taking a turn with the reins while one person slept and the other sat watch. That way they could rest themselves on the move and consequently travel for longer without stopping.

Handen was optimistic about their food stock and thought it would be some time before they had to worry about hunting and scavenging. Water, though infrequent in the wilderness, was not so rare as to pose a major concern. The fugitives were free to concentrate on making as much headway on their pursuers as possible.

Boredom was, of course, a problem. They had swapped most of their stories over the first few days. Handen had regaled his companions with his seemingly endless adventures as an immortal, and Azron, in turn, had told them about his days growing up in Port Town, some of the interesting people he had met and stolen from, and some of the interesting places he had been to and robbed. Bip, who up until several months ago had led an extraordinarily normal life, was content to tell of the peaceful times he had had in Kaneq. (It was a constant source of irritation to Handen that Bip's questing experiences had been relatively harmless and had taken him hardly any time at all, while his own had been unreasonably challenging and had lasted several lifetimes.)

As the days rolled by, however, the stories had run out, and the trio had lapsed into long silences. Handen, quiet by nature, didn't mind the lack of conversation, and Bip, who had already spent months traveling with the former Hostilities Advisor, had grown used to long periods of silence. Azron was of a different opinion. He found the silence tedious and awkward. He liked the quiet in the right circumstances—like when he was in someone else's house uninvited—but when he was off duty (as he liked to think of it) he preferred to chatter or whistle or even just listen to others talking. The long uneventful quiet of the wilderness was almost unbearable to his city-boy instincts, and he found himself yearning for overcrowded streets and loud, inarticulate ramblings.

Azron sighed and tried to start up a conversation again.

"So," he began. "If you were an animal, what kind of animal would you be?"

"Cat," said Bip.

"Wolf," said Handen.

Azron waited for elaboration. "Any particular reason why?" he asked after a time.

"No."

"Not really."

Azron clucked his tongue. "Well you two are a right barrel of laughs, ain't you? Very good company, I must say."

Bip breathed out heavily. "Okay then, Azron, what kind of animal would you be?"

"Well, I was going to say cat," said Azron, "but you've already said that, haven't you?"

"So? Can't we both be cats?"

"No! That's not how the game works! You're s'posed to think of animal and then say why you'd want to be it, and that's s'posed to tell us all a little bit about yourself, innit?"

Bip sat silent for a while. "Don't see why we can't both be cats," he mumbled.

Azron sighed and turned back to his steering, rolling a cigarette expertly in one hand, steadying the reins with the other.

"Well, why don't we play the question game again, then?" he said after a while.

"Is that the one where you think of something and we've got to ask questions until we guess what it is?" said Handen.

"Yeah, that's the one."

"Okay, then, go for it."

Azron thought for a moment and then grinned. "Okay, I've got one. What am I?"

"Are you an animal?" ventured Bip.

"Yep."

"Are you a cat?"

Azron's face clouded over. He turned back to his steering.

They rode on for some hours in silence. For a while Bip amused himself by rechecking the inventory of his reprogrammed acorns. There were still quite a few left, ranging from the useful—such as the SWORD and SHIELD acorns, which would be handy should he ever lose Brian—to the more everyday such as the ROPE and UMBRELLA acorns. There was even an ARMCHAIR acorn, but Bip couldn't really see that being very useful in the near future.

Eventually Bip grew tired of his inventory and began to drift off to sleep. Soon the only sound bar the occasional squawk of a vulture was Bip's gentle, rhythmic snoring.

More hours passed as they rode into the late afternoon. Sunset would not be for another five hours.

Eventually they swapped places, moving Bip onto the steering, Azron onto watch, and allowing Handen to get some rest in the back. It wasn't long before the adventurer was picking up where Bip had left off, snoring steadily into the ovenish day.

Bip yawned to clear his head, keeping the horses in a steady trot until they had regained the energy to pick up the pace a little. Azron put his head in his hand and sighed.

"I'm bored," he said. "Bored, bored, bored."

"Why don't you have another cigarette?" said Bip, who'd noticed the thief had been smoking less than usual, which was to say a cigarette did not hang constantly from his lips.

"Pacing myself, aren't I?" said the thief, glumly. "Running low on 'baccy."

Bip noticed they were heading toward what looked like a canyon. The ground ramped down, and walls of earth rose slowly on either side. He considered going around it, but then realized that it would probably add unnecessary hours to their journey. Handen—whose sense of danger was more finely tuned than either of his companions'—would have insisted they went around. He would have realized, with a soldier's view, that the sloping walls of the canyon would make an excellent ambush point, especially if you wanted to surprise a single, lightly defended wagon. Bip, who had been lulled by the sheer emptiness of the Dozantyne Shrub, sensed and foresaw no danger at all. He headed to the mouth of the canyon without a second thought.

Azron was too wrapped up in his own grumpiness to offer any useful advice. He didn't even react when the rising walls of the canyon began to cast a dark shadow over the wagon.

"Bored, bored, bored," he muttered again.

Bip paid him no attention. His time with Handen had improved his instincts a little, and he was beginning to wonder if he should have skirted around the canyon after all. As the sun began its descent behind the horizon, the canyon had taken on a distinctly menacing feel. Bip's hand went uneasily to the hilt of Brian.

The thief, still distracted by his own gloom, cried out in exasperation. "I just wish something would happen!"

As if to grant his wish, a shrill and birdlike cry echoed around the base of the canyon, followed by a deep rumbling. Bip pulled the horses to a stop as, not far in the distance, a small avalanche of rocks rolled across the canyon floor. Though the rock pile wasn't large, they would still have to clear it before they could move forward. A deadly silence had descended throughout the canyon.

Bip jumped as he felt a hand on his shoulder. He turned to the alert eyes of Handen.

"What's going on?" said the adventurer. Bip saw the gleam of Handen's flintlock pistola in the dwindling light of the evening. He was ready for trouble.

"There was an avalanche ahead of us," whispered Bip.

Handen looked around quickly, taking in their surroundings. "Can we turn around?" he said.

Bip looked about. He had ridden, unwittingly, into a narrow part of the canyon where turning the wagon around would be difficult and slow going. A sinking feeling dragged at Bip's stomach. He suddenly knew they had ridden into an ambush. He glanced up at sides of the canyon and saw hunched figures silhouetted against the approaching evening. They appeared to be armed with spears.

"What are they?" whispered Azron.

"Don't look at them," said Handen. "It might just be that we've encroached on their territory. If we back away, they might leave us alone."

There was another birdlike cry that preceded a heavy, badly made spear thumping into the ground in front of the horses. The mounts reared and whinnied nervously as the spear vibrated in the earth.

"...or maybe not," finished Handen.

There was another birdcall. It appeared to be a challenge.

"Okay, hero, what do we do now?" said Azron.

Handen looked about again. "Too many of them," he said. "I could get out of this one okay, but I doubt if you two could."

"That's reassuring," said the thief. He seemed to have cheered up a bit now that they were in the face of peril.

"What do we do?" Bip said.

"They want us to surrender, that much is clear, otherwise they would've attacked by now." Handen rubbed his bristly chin thoughtfully. "It's our only viable cause of action."

"You can't be serious," scoffed the thief.

"I am," Handen said. "I say we let ourselves be taken. There's a chance we can bargain our way out of this."

THE TRIO STOOD BACK to back at the tall wooden post set into the ground. Heavy ropes bound them, and kindling was being stacked at their feet. All around them, their captors danced jerkily to the beat of a flat-sounding bongo.

"Nice one, mate," said Azron. "Bargain our way out, yeah?"

Handen didn't reply. He had been hoping that they would be taken before their assailants' leader and questioned. He had been fairly confident that, if so, he would be able to talk them out of trouble. That had not been the case, however. The group that had captured them didn't seem to have a leader. Instead they had just manhandled the trio to what was obviously their home ground and tied them abruptly to the suspicious-looking post standing in the center.

Several bonfires had been lit around the grounds so that everything could be seen clearly against the wilderness night, revealing ramshackle huts and ubiquitous piles of guano. The trio had been able to get a good look at their captors. Handen recognized them as vulards, bizarre buzzard-like creatures who had only limited intelligence. Their vocabulary was extremely small, and they were usually content to hang around in their scruffy gangs waiting for other creatures to die so they could eat them. Handen wondered what had inspired their uncharacteristic display of hostility. Bip would have been able to tell him, would have been able to imagine the wicked whispers that had passed through their feathered ears.

He looked at the madly dancing vulards again. They were a sort of inverted cousin of the harpy, with the hunched and oily body of a bird but with the limbs of a man. From the white cluster of feathers at their shoulders, long pink necks warbled toward small, bullet heads with hooked, wicked-looking beaks. With their necks withdrawn, the vulards stood at roughly four feet in height. With their necks extended, however, they towered even over Azron.

The vulards cawed and shrieked continuously, working themselves into a frenzy, the significance of which was lost on their prisoners. Their intentions, however, were perfectly clear. For reasons unapparent, Bip, Handen, and Azron were to be burned at the stake. As if to clarify the point, the vulards began chanting one of the few words they seemed to know. Their voices were harsh and raspy, like a duck with a bad head cold.

"Burn! Burn! Burn! "

"Oh dear," said Bip glumly.

"Ideas, anyone?" asked Azron.

They had all been disarmed when they were captured, but Handen, who had more knives secured about his person at any one time than a well-prepared chef might own in his entire career, had managed to conceal a few of his smaller blades. He worked one of the daggers that he had hidden in his sleeve free and carefully—so as not to drop the weapon or draw attention to himself—began to saw at the rope around his wrists.

"I'm working on something," he said through the side of his mouth. "But I'm going to need a distraction."

"Bip?" said Azron. "Think you can explode anything?"

Bip nodded down at the dry kindling at their feet. "I don't think it would be a good idea to risk it," he said. "We might just be doing our new friends a favor."

Handen tried to increase the pace of his sawing. He was gradually cutting through the ropes, but not at an encouraging rate. The frenzy of the vulards seemed to be increasing to a climax.

"If anyone has any ideas for a distraction, now's the time to tell me," said Handen. "How about a naked woman with an axe?" said Azron.

"Yeah, that'd do," Handen replied distractedly. That was when he heard the war cry.

Xharon: Warrior Princess

I t was a shrill yodel, sudden and piercing in the relative piece of the Shrub. It rose from a teeth-clenching shriek to an ear-splitting trill and wavered between the two rapidly, like some alarm clock from hell.

The bongo playing stopped abruptly, and the vulards ceased their dancing and turned to look at the newcomer with open puzzlement etched into their beaks.

Standing on a boulder just on the outskirts of the bonfire light was a woman. Abundantly a woman. It was hard not to notice the various parts that qualified her as a woman because she did, at first glance, appear to be naked. She was not, however, but the clothing she did wear—a leather thong under a thin chainmail miniskirt and a slim-strapped bra decorated with metal studs—left very little to the imagi-nation. The only part of the stranger's body that seemed to be appro-priately covered was the bottom of her legs, concealed by knee-high boots with impractically high heels.

It wasn't until the woman stopped screaming and Handen got a proper look at her face that he realized that "woman" was not a wholly accurate term. The stranger was closer to being a girl, barely out of her teens. Fiery eyes glittered from a pale face sprayed with a smattering of freckles. Full lips twisted in a feral snarl. A leather head-band held back long red hair that hung nearly to the woman's waist.

Not ginger, not auburn, thought Handen, *but actually red.*

She was, indeed, holding an axe. In fact, she was holding two. The battle-axes, lightweight and designed to be used one handed, appeared ridiculously over-sized in comparison to the small frame of the girl, and Handen, with the cynical mind of a fighter, doubted she'd be able to use them to full effect. He was forced to reconsider his notion when, once again screaming her bizarre war cry, the girl began to twirl the axes in a complex lattice of metal in front of her body. The axes seemed to pass from hand to hand without pause until each arm and weapon became a blur of silvery movement.

The birdmen looked at each other in confusion. Whatever they had expected from this night, shrieking warrior women appearing from nowhere hadn't been part of it.

The redheaded girl ceased her weapons display, throwing the axes carelessly to her sides, and somersaulted forward with balletic grace. She landed lightly and began cartwheeling and flip-flopping toward the vulards, who stood helplessly, still unsure of how to react to the threat.

Her attack might have been a complete success if not for that fact that, as she landed from a complex flip, the heel on one of her boots snapped off. A look of sudden shock replaced the girl's fierce warrior snarl as she fell unexpectedly to the side, twisting her ankle as she went.

Her pale face went even paler, and she dropped to her knees and clutched the injured ankle tightly.

"Ouchouchouchouchouch!" she said.

Both vulards and prisoners alike were shocked into silence. Every-one, it seemed, had been holding their breath.

"Ouch?" Handen heard Azron say. "Who actually says 'ouch'?"

His question was answered for him as the stranger continued her litany of pain. "OuchouchouchOUCH!"

Handen dismayed. At their potential rescuer's display of skill, his hopes for escape had risen, but now, as the warrior sat clutching her ankle and hissing through clenched teeth, it was clear that things weren't going to go in their favor.

The girl cried out again. "Buggerbuggerbugger!" The unladylike swearing rubbed oddly against her plummy accent.

She was too wrapped up in her pain to realize she had been surrounded by the vulards, whose confusion had quickly given way to malicious hostility. She looked up from her ankle and took in the spears leveled at her head.

"Oh…" she said. "Oh, bugger."

"PLEASED TO ME YOU," said Bip as the strange girl was tied up next to him. He felt that he should at least introduce himself to the person he was going to be dying next to. "I'm Bip Plunkerton, that's Handen Strike, and the tall chap is Azron Bezron."

"That's Azron Bezron, Diamond Geezer (1st Class)," interjected Azron smoothly. Bip had a feeling that if Azron had been able to, he would have smoothed back his hair.

"Pleased to meet you, I'm sure," said the girl sulkily. Suddenly she seemed to straighten up, as if remembering herself. "I am Xharon, Warrior Princess," she said.

Handen caught Azron's eye. The thief shrugged.

"That's an interesting name," said Bip. His voice caught and cracked oddly, like an adolescent barging his way through puberty. He had become aware of Xharon's flesh pressing against his own and was suddenly and absurdly glad they were all tied to a post together. In his busy life of avoiding work, Bip had never really had time for girlfriends. He didn't think he had ever been this close to a woman who wasn't his mum.

Xharon's shoulders slumped. "Not that it matters now," she said. "I've cocked things up a bit, haven't I?"

"Don't be so hard on yourself," said Handen. "You couldn't have taken them all on." Bip noticed that his friend's voice sounded distracted. He correctly assumed that the adventurer had gone back to sawing at the ropes on his hands.

"I bally well could have!" said Xharon, hotly. "They were just lucky, that's all!"

"Fair enough," said Handen. "Not that it matters now." The vulards were resuming their chanting and dancing. It would not take them long to reach their culmination once more. "If somebody doesn't cause a distraction soon, we're all going to die."

"Well, that's not exactly true, is it?" said Azron. "You can't die, can you?"

"No," said Handen. "I guess I'll just have to sit here and burn horribly until they figure that out, won't I?"

Azron sucked his breath in sharply through his teeth. "Ooo. Yeah. 'Course. Didn't think of that." The thief was suddenly very glad he wasn't immortal. He could imagine scorched nerve endings healing and re-healing only to be burnt away again in perpetual agony.

Bip said nothing. An idea had occurred to him. He didn't have any weapons concealed on him and daren't use his psyence less he hasten their demise, but there was one option that hadn't occurred to him until now. He felt for the bag of reprogrammed acorns in his pocket. If he could get one into his mouth and spit it, he might just provide all the distraction necessary for Handen to cut them free. He grinned as his mind's eye saw the reaction of the primitive birdmen to an organic armchair suddenly growing in the middle of them. He reached his tied-up hands down to his pocket and began rummaging for the bag. He tried not to get too excited as he finally snagged it and pulled it, inch by inch, from his trousers.

His hopes were dashed as swiftly as they had appeared as the bag was snagged out of his grasp by the gnarled hand of a vulard. The bird-like creature stared at Bip accusingly with its beady eyes before turning his attention to the contents of the bag. Its mouth fell open with an astonished squawk as it saw what was inside.

"Seeeeeds!" it cawed with croaking delight.

The entire ritual stopped. Every vulard had turned to the one holding the bag, which, by the worried look in his eye, appeared to be regretting its outburst.

"Seeeds?"

"Seeeeds?"

"Seeeeeds!"

Without warning, the whole tribe rushed the vulard with the acorns. There was a riotous scuffle as every one of the birdmen tried to grab the bag at once. Predictably, the flimsy sacking bag ripped to pieces under the strain, and the acorns scattered across the ground.

Without a pause, the vulards began bobbing their long necks toward the ground, trying desperately to scoop up the morsels in their long beaks. Only a few were successful, cawing triumphantly as they gobbled down what was apparently a vulard delicacy.

Unthinkingly, Bip, Azron and Handen had all squinted their eyes shut. Xharon looked confused.

"What?" she said. "What's happening?"

"Wait and see," said Handen through clenched teeth.

The vulards stopped their cackling. A few of the birdmen—the ones who had successfully nabbed the seeds—bore expressions of extreme puzzlement. Suddenly, one of them hiccupped loudly and then glanced around in confused panic. Without warning, the bird-like creature suddenly exploded in a mess of gore and feathers. Where it had stood was now a large, comfortable looking armchair made entirely of wood and leaves.

Before the rest of the tribe could react, there were more shrieks of terror and horrified surprise from their comrades. Carnage of the most bizarre kind began to befall the vulard tribe. Here a creature warbled in panic before a wooden sword blade erupted messily from its chest. Elsewhere a vulard came to a nasty end as a wooden umbrella unfurled in its neck, sending its head flying into the air with a popping noise that might have been humorous in other circumstances. One of the birdmen gagged helplessly as a large length of rope uncoiled rapidly from its mouth.

Amidst the chaos, the still-healthy vulards began to run in every direction, leaving their inexplicably dying comrades behind lest they should suffer a similar fate.

The four prisoners squinted in sympathy for their unfortunate captors. "As far as distractions go," said Azron, "that was a doozy."

IT HAD TAKEN them longer than they would have liked to turn the wagon around and ride back out of the canyon. They had to tread the horses carefully in the dark; the possibility of breaking a wheel on the rocks or, worse, a horse's leg in a pothole was too great. Xharon had helped, leading her own horse ahead of them at a slow pace, limping on her freshly bound ankle.

Handen had been impressed by the girl's steed, a shiny black gelding that looked to be from thoroughbred stock and stood at least fifteen hands high. She had named it Prancer, which seemed a little inappropriate for the heavily muscled charger.

After some endeavour, they eventually made camp with their backs to a high rocky outcrop. They were unsure whether the vulards would regroup and come looking for them. Handen doubted it but would stand watch anyway, determined not to give them the advantage of surprise. Xharon, though reluctant at first, accepted the offer to camp with them.

Now they sat around the campfire again, slightly exhausted from their ordeal and looking forward to the slowly cooking meat and the brewing coffee, which the vulards had, oddly, left untouched.

It was Azron who spoke first. "So," he said to Xharon. "What brings a nice young girl like you to a wilderness like this?"

Xharon narrowed her eyes slightly at the thief's tone. "I came to seek adventure," she said.

"Well, good luck to you, miss," said Azron. "Those bird guys are the first things we've seen in ages. Nothing else but dust and shrub for miles."

"I know," said Xharon downheartedly. "It's not at all like in the books. "

"Books?" said Bip.

Xharon sighed. "You read the stories, you know. They tell of ancient beasts and peril in the southlands. I hear all sorts of things about rogue orcen tribes and elfen freedom fighters. And so far, nothing. Not a sausage."

"You should have come a thousand years ago," Handen said under his breath.

"Except for you fellows, of course," Xharon added. "What did those funny little bird things want with you anyway?"

"To kill us, apparently," said Handen.

"But why?"

Handen chuckled mirthlessly. "I stopped trying to figure that one out a long time ago."

Bip held his tongue. He did not want to upset things further by mentioning the interfering deviousness of Mr. Random.

Xharon accepted a cup of coffee gratefully. "So, what are you chaps doing out here in the Shrub?" she said.

The three men looked at each other for a while, and then, sighing, knowing that at some point he'd probably have to stab himself again, Handen began telling their collective story.

Xharon listened intently, sitting with the wide-eyed wonder of a child. As he recounted their tale, Handen felt the uneasy suspicion that Xharon really enjoyed stories—particularly stories such as theirs. He didn't even have to stab himself to prove he was immortal; the girl just seemed to accept it as if it were the most natural thing in the world. He wrapped up the story with the ambush by the vulards and a rather anticlimactic "...and the rest you know."

Xharon just sat there for a while, eyes wide, staring off into some make-believe world.

"Incredible," she breathed. "Amazing! You're all actually on a quest? A real life quest?"

The three fugitives exchanged glances. "Yeah, I suppose," said Azron.

"A real-life race against time, where the fate of the world hangs in the balance?"

"Yes?" said Bip, nervously.

"Brilliant! Can I come? You don't know how long I've waited for something like this! *Ohpleaseohpleaseohplease!*"

Handen coughed. "I don't think that's a very good idea," he said.

For a moment, Xharon had the look of a freshly kicked puppy. This look was quickly taken over by a flash of irritation. "Why not?" she snapped.

"You don't seem to understand," said Handen, patiently. "This isn't some thrill-seeking adventure for honor and glory. This is important. If we don't get to where we need to go in time, people will die. Everyone will die. And there are people trying to stop us and miles of hostile terrain to cover."

"All the more reason why you need my help." Xharon sniffed, crossing her arms over her chest.

Handen sighed. "What makes you think we need help?" he said.

"Well, correct me if I'm wrong, but weren't you the ones about to be cooked alive by overgrown pigeons?"

"That's a fair point, that," said Azron, and Handen was forced to concede. Romantic or not, another fighter would be useful if they ran into trouble again.

He held up his hands. "Okay, okay. As long as you pull your weight, you can ride with us. As far as the capital and then you're on your own."

Xharon looked crestfallen. "You're going back to Argustin?"

"Yes. Why?"

"I've just come from there!" she said testily.

She looked around at the curious faces of her new companions. "I did mention I was a princess, didn't I?"

The three fugitives merely stared at her, awaiting elaboration.

"It's my full title. I'm Xharon DeChambre, Princess of Argustin. I'm the Emperor's niece."

HANDEN, Bip, and Azron stood huddled together away from the light of the campfire. Back at the wagon, Xharon began rubbing down her horse, singing in a faltering soprano that carried flatly through the night air.

"She's the bloody *princess*!" said Azron.

"I don't understand," said Bip. "What's she doing out here if she's a princess?"

"She's young and she wants adventure," said Handen, shrugging as if that explained everything.

"She's the *bloody* princess!" Azron repeated.

"She knows the Emperor is after us. I don't understand why she wants to ride with us if her own uncle wants to see us captured," Bip said.

"Perhaps she's just an angry rich girl rebelling against her peers. She wouldn't be the first," said Handen calmly.

"*She's* the bloody princess!"

"Yes, we know! Now please stop saying that!"

"But we could be well in here! Well in! I bet she's bloody loaded!"

Mentally, Handen agreed. The craftsmanship of her weaponry was exquisite, and her horse was fit for a king. Or a princess. He had no reason to doubt that the girl was definitely from one of the noble families. Either that or a thief and a con artist.

"Azron, why are you so convinced she actually is the princess and not some madwoman with an expensive horse?"

"I've seen pictures, haven't I?" said Azron. "She's the *bloody princess*." He stopped and thought for a while. "Mind you, she had more clothes on in the pictures I've seen."

"Well, this is good news," said Handen.

"Too right!" Azron grinned. "I bet she's bloody loaded!"

"No. What I mean is, if she's the Emperor's niece, then she should have no problem getting us in to see him."

"Of course!" said Bip.

"Which means no climbing walls, no wrestling past guards, no bribing city officials. We just walk right in."

"Well, I suppose that's good, too," said Azron, hesitantly. "But I do have one more question. One I've been meaning to ask you guys for a little while now, sort of thing."

"Yes?"

"Well, if it's the Emperor you want to see, and the Emperor wants to catch you, then why don't you just, you know, give yourselves up?"

Bip blinked rapidly. He was ashamed to admit that that particular course of action, obvious as it was, had not occurred to him.

"Firstly," said Handen, "there's no guaranteeing the Emperor would grant us an audience. Could be that he just wants to see us safely locked up. Secondly, even if we were granted an audience, then he's less likely to believe the reasoning of two condemned prisoners. No, we have to go to him ourselves—it's the only way to lend any credibility to our story."

Azron shrugged. "Makes sense," he said. "And the young princess could be just what we need to talk to the Emperor on a one-to-one basis, yeah?"

"That's right," said Handen.

"So she's coming with us, then?" said Bip. He tried to keep his voice cool, but a waver of hot excitement still escaped.

"Yes. She's coming with us."

THE TRIO RETURNED to the campfire where Xharon stood waiting with her fists on her hips.

"So you're having me along, then?" she said.

The three fugitives nodded in unison.

"Great!" said Xharon, and jumped up and down on the spot for a while in what appeared to be some sort of happy dance. Bip found himself hypnotized by various jigglings as the dance went on. After she had finished, she looked back at her new companions. "And do we have to go back to Argustin?"

"Listen very carefully," said Handen, slowly. "We must be granted a personal audience with the Emperor. He may be our only chance to save the world."

The adventurer watched as the words sank into the young princess's impressionable mind. "Saving the world," she breathed softly.

"Yes. The whole world," said Handen.

"No problem," said Xharon, a wide grin lighting up her face. "Uncle Tommy always likes to see me." The princess hunkered down in her bedroll and gazed at the stars overhead through eyes glazed with excitement. "Saving the world," she muttered to herself.

"Uncle Tommy?" whispered Azron. Handen shrugged.

Interlude: The Rescue Party

Not for the first time that day, Bailey wished he were still in bed. He stared through the electric gray clouds to where the weak light of the sun shone. He still found the position of the flat silvery disk both surprising and a little frightening. He was not used to seeing the outside world before noon. It felt alien.

His perception wasn't helped by his lack of hangover. As far back as he could remember, Bailey had always been a little hungover each morning, but seven days of stone-cold sobriety had left him feeling clear-headed and alert. He didn't like it. It was like being plunged suddenly into a cold bath.

What he liked even less than all that was being out in the middle of the Ice Plains with a big spear, a man who was quite obviously mad, and seventeen other frightened and confused youths.

The people of Kaneq had learned about the end of the world a week ago. A town meeting had been called in the square, and the elders had flooded into the Stadium of Address. The news had been broken by Tenbon, who had spoken slowly in her somber, deep tone of the upcoming destruction of Bersch. To her right, Truggle had sat staring into unknown voids as if his thoughts were elsewhere. The crowd had listened, first confused, then frightened, until a roar of despair had filled the heart of Kaneq.

Bailey remembered feeling sick suddenly, an odd mixture of dread and delight that Bip, who had vanished mysteriously so many months ago, had in fact left in an attempt to reach civilization.

When the crowd finally came to an uneasy silence, Tenbon told them of her plan, the last hope for Kaneq: one last excursion to the mainland, this time in numbers of dozens rather than just one or two. She had left the crowd a day to think about it before she would call a meeting asking for volunteers.

It had not taken Kaneq's citizens long to come to the same conclusion Bip had come to when given the option of saving the world: that there was no real choice. If you left to venture into the wilderness, it was likely that you might die. If you stayed and hoped for the best, death was inevitable. So many of Kaneq's population had found themselves volunteering. Heroes by necessity.

Many had been turned away, of course, being too young or too old or holding a position deemed too important in the town to abandon. Those who did not or could not volunteer helped in as many ways as possible; farmers gave up produce for the cause, bakers baked stacks of sustaining travel bread, tailors began fashioning winter wear, and blacksmiths began forging weapons and armor.

For the volunteers who had been accepted, a rigorous and complex training regime had been drawn up, bouncing them between senior hunters and psyentists. Because there were so many students, more time had to be allocated for training than the period Bip had been allowed—but many, Rynford especially, doubted that so large a number of students could be brought up to an acceptable level of development in so little time. And so training started earlier, students were pushed harder. Those who could not cope with the pace had become bedridden, drastically culling the number of trainees.

Of the hundreds who had bravely volunteered, only half had made it into the second week of training. The Kaneqian people, though strong in spirit, had bodies rendered weak by years of easy living. Of the half that continued the training process, most were either the young or those employed in areas where physical exertion was a matter of course.

Bailey looked around at the volunteers around him, Kaneqian men and women, formally farmers or marketers, suddenly hefting heavy furs and spears in the inhumane climate of the Ice Plains. All of the volunteers, their noses uniformly red with the cold, were staring intently at Rynford, who was explaining once again the importance of not being killed.

They were standing on the cusp of a large, and of course, snowy dale. At the bottom, a herd of snowcows grazed ceaselessly on the ice-brittle shrubbery that always held a tenuous grasp on survival in the Ice Plains. Rynford rounded up his speech and asked for a volunteer to carry out the day's lesson. As usual, no one was in a hurry to step forward. Rynford sighed and scanned the crowd. Eventually, he pointed at a student.

"You," he said simply.

The crowd parted to reveal "Half-Brick" Thompson, who was staring ahead with his usual vacant contentment and clasping his spear the wrong way round.

Bailey was surprised that he himself had survived the training process thus far. Having spent the entirety of his teenage years drinking, smoking, and generally lying about, the wonderful machinery of his body had been transformed into something that coughed and spluttered frequently when pushed too hard. He was young, though, and was slowly adapting to the harsh physical and mental pressures of the training regime. He was really surprised, however, that Half-Brick had made it this far without impaling himself on his own spear.

"Now," continued Rynford, "using the methods I have just explained, I want you to go and kill that snowcow—the one with the limp that is standing away from the rest of the herd. Do you see it?"

Half-Brick peered into the valley base. "It's a cow," he said.

"I'll take that as a yes," Rynford said. "Now, as I told you, circle around the prey and stalk it from behind its line of vision, keeping downwind of the rest of the herd. Then, when close enough, jab your spear into its underbelly and keep pushing until it loses balance and topples over. Then you'll be ready for the kill. Right?"

"Right," said Half-Brick.

"Okay!" said Rynford. "Now go!"

With a blood-curdling scream, Half-Brick began running down the valley slope, dropping his spear behind him as he went. Several of the volunteers put their hands over their eyes as the farm boy sprinted toward the grazing beast. Rynford looked on in a mix of pained disappointment and horrified disbelief.

Half-Brick continued to charge and ran head-first into the prone beast's ribs. The volunteers let out a collective empathetic hiss. Half-Brick was hard headed, but no match for the bulk of the snowcow. The farm boy stood for a moment, a stunned look in his eye. Then, with a grace he could never have mustered intentionally, collapsed unconscious into the snow. The snowcow looked around with typically bovine indifference, then went back to grazing as if nothing had happened.

Rynford let out a long sigh. "Right," he said. "I'm going to need a couple of volunteers to retrieve the Thompson boy, and then we'll get on with the lesson, shall we?"

Bailey shook his head and wished, once more, that he were still in bed.

11

The Dead Wood

A warm breezed caressed the balding pate of the Shrub, gliding with a futile affection that was neither perceived nor wanted. The soft seduction of the rare wilderness breezes was nothing compared to the constant smothering love of the everyday sunshine. The earth baked, hardboiled and loyal, withered and aged, staring up to a lover as young and old as the sky itself. The wind moaned, but she'd get over it.

The epic love triangle was lost on Bip. For him, the landscape had ceased to hold interest. A view more animal and human was occupying all of his attention, and with his mouth dry and his stomach clenched, he was grateful once again that Azron had the reins; Bip doubted he could have held a steady course if his life had depended on it.

Xharon sat perched upon Prancer in a way that was both pert and fluid, both rigid and languid. She moved and swayed with the trotting of the horse as though dancing to some unheard lullaby. Bip took in the arch of her pale shoulders, burned slightly by the sun, a few patches of pink that complemented the long red hair that fell almost to her waist. He was able to study the slightly plump line of her hips and follow the occasional, maddening bead of sweat that would crawl slowly down the princess's back and collect around smooth, oily buttocks.

Bip hadn't realized, but a large slibber of drivel had wormed slowly down his chin.

It wasn't love, but it was the burning libido-fueled hormone charge that passed for love at seventeen. It didn't matter to Bip—perhaps didn't even register to him—that Xharon was not particularly beautiful, that her teeth were slightly bucked and her eyes slightly squint. It didn't matter that she had a tendency to laugh like a troubled gopher and talk about nothing but horses for seemingly hours. What mattered to Bip was that, of all the girls he had ever known or seen in his travels, Xharon was wearing the least amount of clothing.

Later in his life, Bip would reflect that this was perhaps a shallow basis for falling in love, but there and then, Bip would have happily beaten himself to death with his own shoe if Xharon had told him to —simply because she seemed to be wearing nothing more than a series of leather belts. It would also occur to him later in life, when the fires of teenage libido had been doused somewhat, that this was a rather fundamental and ridiculous flaw in the male psyche.

"Nuh?" said Bip as he felt Azron's elbow nudge into his ribs.

"I said, 'It almost makes you wish you'd been born a horse, doesn't it?'" said the thief, and nodded suggestively at Xharon's saddle region.

Bip turned to Azron's leering grin and felt a blush charge furiously over his face. "I didn't mean to stare," he mumbled.

"Stare?" chuckled Azron. "I thought your eyes were going to fly out of your head!"

"Well, don't you think she's pretty?" said Bip.

Azron rubbed his hairy chin thoughtfully. "My tastes are a touch more cosmopolitan," he said, eventually. "It's not the figure of the girl that matters—it's the figures in her dowry."

"Azron, that's awful!" hissed Bip reproachfully.

"Oh yes?" The thief grinned. "And you're taken by her sparkling personality, are you?"

Bip looked at the floor, feeling shame that he hadn't the emotional experience to identify or deal with. He looked up to see that Xharon was falling back a little, obviously meaning to talk with the cart riders. The Kaneqian felt a butterfly storm of guilt and panic erupt in the pit of his stomach.

"Talking about anything interesting, chaps?" said Xharon, easing Prancer into a steady trot that perfectly matched the cart's ponderous progress.

Azron grinned widely. "Actually, yes—Bip here was just about to ask you something, isn't that right, Bip?"

Bip gaped and spluttered and finally relented under the guileless curiosity of Xharon's gaze. He tried to think of something clever or disarming to say but—as was usually the case when put under pressure to be dashing—his brain had wandered off somewhere. "I was just wondering where you got your outfit," he said, settling on something that was at least half true.

"It's the battle attire of the Turnmisin swamp she-warriors. They wear this when they go to war," said Xharon, matter-of-factly.

"Really?" said Azron chirpily. "Spend much time in the Turnmisin swamps then, did you?"

Xharon flushed a pretty pink, causing Bip to swallow hard. "Well… no," she said. "I read about them in a book."

Azron nodded as if expecting the reply. "So your only basis that what you are wearing is indeed the common attire of these she-warriors, who dwell in a land covered mostly with poisonous flora and dangerous stinging beasties, is derived from a book?"

Xharon's eyes narrowed. "Yes? What's your point?"

"Oh, nothing, nothing," replied Azron. "Just wondering out loud."

There was an awkward silence that Bip felt compelled to break. "So is that where you learned to fight, then?" he said. "From books?"

"Of course not," said Xharon. "Don't be silly. I've had some of the finest weapons masters in Argustin at my disposal. Uncle Tommy says girls shouldn't fight, but the guards have to teach me if I tell them to. I am a princess, after all."

"Oh, I see," said Bip. He thought desperately for another conversation opener. "So why did you want to fight?"

Xharon rolled her eyes as if Bip had just asked why babies cry or why trees grow upward. "Well, isn't it obvious?" she said. "If one wants to become a warrior princess, then one must at some point become a warrior!"

"Ah," said Bip, and left it at that.

Azron chuckled quietly under his breath. "I think what my silver-tongued mate here meant was, why be a warrior princess at all? Why not just lounge around the palace eating jam or something?"

"You wouldn't understand," said Xharon, glumly. "Royalty is no life for a girl with spirit. There's no excitement, and every day is the same. People treat you as though you're a china plate, and the only ones who talk to you honestly are other royalty, and frankly, I can't stand them. You tell people that you want to be a warrior, and they nod at you patronizingly and say, 'yes ma'am,' like you're just being silly, and the stupid servants wont even let you dress yourself in the mornings, and they let you win at cards all the time, and they won't let you do anything you want to do, and it's enough to make you sick!" Xharon breathed heavily for a while, catching her breath.

Azron and Bip exchanged a stunned glance. The echoes of the princess's rant shivered around the empty Shrub.

"So I ran away," she continued. "To find adventure, or at the very least someone who'll take me seriously."

"It's like I always say," said Azron after a while, "if you can't take a half-naked teenage girl holding an axe seriously, then what can you?"

Xharon narrowed her eyes again. "Are you making fun of me?" she said.

"Who, me?" Azron grinned, his crooked teeth gleaming in the sunlight.

"Well, you'd better not be." The princess sniffed. "Or I'll bally well chop your hands off." She stuck out her tongue and urged Prancer into a canter, leaving the cart behind.

Azron grinned. "I like a girl with spirit," he said.

"Really?" said Bip.

The thief frowned in thought for a moment. "No," he said. "That's not what I meant to say—I meant, 'I like a girl with money.'"

"That's what I thought."

IN THE BACK of the cart, Handen slept fitfully. In his mind, half-dissolved images of memories just under the surface of recollection pulled at and tickled his synapses. The ghosts of dead incidents glided through his mind with clumsy melancholy, hinting at emotions whose relevance and meaning were buried beneath an avalanche of years. Throughout the throng of thought and feeling, a nagging pulse like a vindictive headache throbbed ceaselessly, a thin and brilliant red line in an otherwise murky consciousness. Something was calling to him. Calling to him on a level greater than subconscious but just far enough beyond the conscious to be able to stand up and speak its name. Handen's eyes fluttered open, and he sat bolt upright. He looked about the cart. Nothing had changed since he had drifted off. Azron still had the reins, and Xharon still rode ahead. The cart was still comfortably full with supplies. Bip still seemed to be fixated on Xharon's horse, for some reason. Everything was exactly the same as when he had drifted off—so why did everything feel different?

The former Hostilities Advisor surveyed the horizon. It was the usual unimaginatively flat horizon he had left behind when he'd fallen asleep but now, to the far south, like a mole on an otherwise flawless face, a forest was slowly crawling into view. A force of affirmation hit him suddenly and brilliantly. He knew beyond a shadow of a doubt that whatever was affecting him, pulling at him, was in those woods.

"Turn about, south-east," he said.

Azron looked around, a cigarette loitering from his lower lip. "Well, good morning to you too, mister sunshine. Have a nice kip, did we?"

"Head toward that forest," Handen reiterated.

Azron looked doubtfully at the slithering black mass in the distance. "Are you sure? I thought you said that the forests were probably dangerous."

"I know what I said," snapped Handen. "But this is important. I think there's something there we need to find."

Or something there that I need to find, anyway, added a cynical voice in the adventurer's head.

Azron shrugged and then, putting his fingers in his mouth, let out a piercing whistle. Xharon turned at the sound and galloped over to the cart.

"What's going on?" she said.

"Change of plans, luv," said Azron. "We're heading to that ominous-looking forest over there."

Xharon shielded her eyes from the sun and squinted at the dark wood. "You mean the forest that looks like it might be full to the brim with monsters and demons and horrible things from beyond the boundaries of man's domain?" she said.

"Yeah, that's the one."

"Oh, smashing!" she said, and galloped out back in front.

THEY STOOD on the cusp of the dead forest. The entrance to the pathway was marked by the interlocking boughs of two long-lifeless trees, melded together in an eternal arm-wrestle. Beyond, the gray cadaver leaves omitted the light of the sun, causing a thick, wet darkness more associable with the mouth of a cave than a forest clearing. Along the ground, fossilized pine and bark formed a skeletal carpet, bone-dry with age and neglect, emanating an old and dusty smell. Each rotting trunk chattered in suspicious whispers as countless insects, evolved by their conditions into mutant, sinister things, chittered and skittered through the corpse-like foliage.

The travelers sat in awed silence, each keenly aware of the pervasive doom the dead wood emanated, like a desecrated tomb or a haunted house.

"Wow," breathed Xharon. "This is brilliant."

Azron fetched the warrior princess a disbelieving look and puffed a little harder on the cigarette he still held.

"I'd put that smoke out if I were you," said Handen, distractedly. "This whole place is liable to go up like kindling."

Azron looked around at the dead, dry trees around them, suddenly imagining them alive with fire, burning and vengeful. He stubbed out his half-smoked cigarette and put the remainder behind his ear.

"I'm surprised the trees don't just collapse in on themselves," said Bip.

Handen nodded his agreement. "There's something deeper at work here than nature. I can feel...something else."

As he spoke, a long growl like the grinding of a heavy stone block reverberated from somewhere deep in the forest. Bip gulped, deeply suspicious of what terrible things might choose to live in perpetual blackness.

"I tell you what," said Azron, unease infecting his normally confident tones, "why don't we just go around, eh?"

"I'll second that," said Bip. He felt that something less tangible than yetis and vulards lay beyond the veil of shadow, something all the more terrifying for being half-imagined.

"Oh, come on, chaps!" said Xharon, hefting her twin axes in her hands. "Where's your sense of adventure?"

"I must have left it in my other trousers," mumbled Azron.

"We have to go through," said Handen suddenly, hollowly. "I can't explain it, but we need to go through here."

Azron sighed. "Much as I want go into this highly suspicious and potentially dangerous situation with you, Handen, old chum, I just don't think we'll be able to fit the cart in."

"We'll go in on foot."

"Oh? Oh."

"We'll leave the cart and horses here."

Azron's expression brightened considerably. "Then we'll be needing someone to stay with the horses, yes?"

Handen looked around at the empty horizons of the Dozantyne Shrub. "In case what?" he said sarcastically. "In case they're stolen by a tumbleweed? No. We all go in together."

Xharon descended from her horse with a graceful flip. "Sounds good to me," she said.

"Oh, yes," Azron grumbled. "Absolutely super."

THEY WALKED in single file into the rotten tunnel of the forest clearing, Handen taking the lead and Azron, having hastily volunteered to do so, taking up the rear. The thief was, by no means, a coward, having willingly placed himself in life-threatening situations throughout his career, it was just that he didn't feel right standing in the open while other things creeped in the shadows. He firmly believed that if there was any shadow creeping to be done, it ought to be him doing it.

Bip had fallen in behind Xharon, who strutted behind the determined Handen with a nonchalant readiness.

"Aren't you scared?" said Bip with genuine curiosity.

Xharon turned around and looked at Bip as though he were being naïve and silly. "Of course not," she said. "Why would I be?"

"Well, I don't know," said Bip. "Ghosts? Giant spiders? Huge beasts of improbable ferocity?"

Xharon twirled one of her axes meaningfully. "I'm sure that whatever comes along we'll be able to handle it," she said, confidently.

"Oh, right," said Bip. He guessed that in the books Xharon had read, the heroes or heroines were rarely eaten alive by paradigms of monstrous evil, rarely died screaming hysterically as their insides suddenly became their outsides. He shuddered and tried to brush aside all thoughts of terrible death. It was hard, though, in a place that seemed to whisper sticky threats from its multitude of dark corners.

Somewhere in the dark, a twig snapped. The noise was followed by something that might have been a sinister chuckle. The party froze, Handen drawing his flintlock and bastard sword with streaking quickness, Xharon gripping her axes tightly, Bip's hand flying shakily to the pommel of Brian, and Azron spreading his arms and bending his knees as if preparing to run in any direction. The forest remained quiet. Horribly quiet. After a few minutes that stretched into nightmare eternity, Handen lowered his weapons and began walking forward again. The rest of the group followed, though Bip noticed the pace was slower than before. Even some of Xharon's confident swagger seemed to have departed.

They walked for what seemed like hours, starting at every sudden sound or silhouette that scurried out of sight before it could be properly identified. As they advanced, the gloom in the wood seemed to thicken, and a mournful sort of mist began to cling to the ground, obscuring the view of the forest floor. Still the party advanced, completely silent, led by Handen who marched forward with grim determination, hands hovering ready over his various holsters and scabbards, or clutching trustfully to the oiled leather of his bullwhip.

Soon the pathway they had been traveling across came to a large circular clearing. The space in the forest was walled in on all sides by thick dead growth, and despite the large circumference of the clearing, the daytime sky was still obliterated by a crisscrossing ceiling of branches and leaves.

Handen shivered. Whatever ethereal force had drawn him into the forest in the first place was centered in this clearing. He could feel it like a foot pushing down on his chest. He signaled for the others to stop behind him. Though he had been powerfully drawn to the clearing, the feeling of attraction was not a pleasant one. It was more like the urge to fall asleep in a smoke-filled room—alluring, powerful, but ultimately fatal.

"Wait here," he said, and began walking forward across the mist-covered floor.

The others watched as he approached the center of the clearing, then gasped when, with a startled cry, the immortal dropped out of sight.

HANDEN WAS, at first, completely surprised as the earthen walls, acned with gray, dead roots, rushed upward across his line of sight, interacting dizzily with the plunging sensation in his chest and stomach as he fell toward the darkness below. However, it did not take long for the adventurer's finely-honed survival instincts to kick in. He reached out and grabbed at a thick root, and his fall came to a jolting stop. He hung there for a while, dangling in the darkness over an uncertain drop.

Now what? he thought.

"Hello down there?" a familiar voice called.

Handen looked up to see the silhouettes of three heads looking down on him from a faint circle of light. Apparently, he hadn't fallen as far as he thought he had, maybe twenty feet or so.

"I'm all right," he called up.

"What's down there?" came the voice. Handen recognized it as Bip's.

"I don't know. I can't see," replied Handen.

"Hold on, mate." Azron's voice this time. "We'll have you out of there in a jiffy!" At the top of the hole, which had turned out to be only six feet or so in diameter, Bip, Azron and Xharon knelt, all thoughts of horrible forest-dwelling creatures temporarily forgotten.

"What do we do now?" said Xharon.

"Well," said Bip. "There's some rope in the cart. One of us will have to go back and get it."

The trio looked uncertainly at the dark path they had come from.

"I'll go," said Xharon, and began jogging the way they had come.

The thief and the doomsayer watched her for a while.

"One of us should go with her," said Bip, making to stand up. He was stopped by a hand on his shoulder.

"Yeah, you're right," said Azron, using Bip's momentum to launch quickly to his feet. "You stay here, and I'll be back before you know it."

"Wait a minute!" Bip called to Azron's retreating back. The Kaneqian sat back with a huff. He couldn't leave Handen alone, of course, but he felt suddenly vulnerable sitting by himself surrounded by the twisted trees.

Down in the hole, Handen managed to secure a foothold in the earthen walls, taking the strain away from his hands. He looked about him, trying to judge what the purpose of the hole was. His gaze was inevitably drawn to the darkness below him. As he looked, the terrible drawing sensation, the foot on his chest, became suddenly unbearable.

The former Hostilities Advisor had to fight the urge to drop willingly into the unknown.

"Bip?" he called.

The silhouette of Bip's head appeared over the lip of the hole. "Yes?"

"Pass me a torch down, will you?"

Bip's head disappeared as he retrieved one of the pre-rolled torches from his pack and dipped it into the hole. Handen caught it easily and held it in his teeth. He fumbled for a match in his coat pocket and, finding one, struck it on his bristly chin, bristly from weeks of travel, and lit the cloth end of the torch. He winced slightly as the heat scorched his face, then dropped the torch beneath him. The torch did not fall as far as he expected, only twirled through the air for a couple of seconds before coming to rest on what appeared to be a white stone floor. The fall was only another fifteen feet or so, one Handen could easily make without even twisting an ankle. Without hesitation, the immortal let go of the root and dropped to the surface below.

He landed with a horrible crunching noise and for one worrying moment wondered if he had misjudged the length of the drop and broken his bones. He was nearly right; he had broken some bones. They just didn't belong to him. All around him, what he had assumed to be a stone floor was in fact a thick carpet of bones—some animal, some humanoid, but all gray and brittle with age. Handen shuddered with disgust as he looked down at the small human skull his boots had crushed.

Pulling himself together, the adventurer scanned the wide cave he now found himself in. The torchlight reflected from hundreds of hollow skulls set into the sloping earthen walls like cobblestones. At the opposite end of the room, the bones were piled up in some sort of shrine. The pulling sensation once again put its foot down on Handen's chest, and he found himself powerfully drawn to the construction. He could no more stop himself walking over to the bone pile than he could stop himself blinking in bright light.

He traversed the sloping hill of bones until he reached its pinnacle, then gazed with dread wonder at what he found there. Before him was a circular pool of what might charitably be called water, though its consistency and color was like that of melted toffee. The stagnant pool gave off a stench that put Handen in mind of spoiled meat. He had to stop himself from gagging.

Understanding hit Handen like a thousand epiphanies. He knew beyond a shadow of a doubt that the pool before him was the source of the ill feeling throughout the dead forest, was perhaps the very source of the forest itself. He understood that before him was the fountain of death.

He felt a sudden rush of fear and excitement, perhaps the most potent excitement he had felt in centuries. Here was a way out. Here was the sweet release he had dreamed of throughout his long incarceration.

He froze as a seductive whisper sounded at the back of his mind.

Drink. Drink.

A faint horror tingled Handen's spine as a dry and powerful thirst climbed suddenly into his throat. For a moment, the sticky pool at his feet seemed to be the most appealing thing he had ever seen. He bent down to the water, undeterred by a fat bubble that rose and popped beneath his nose, releasing a stench like dead animals.

Drink. Drink.

It might have ended for Handen there and then, leaving his flesh to rot and his bones to merge with the thousands of others, had not another voice interrupted him.

"Handen?" called Bip, his voice distant and echoing in the weird acoustics of the death cave. "Handen? Is everything okay?"

Handen shook himself like a man emerging from a particularly engrossing daydream. "Yes," he called back. "Everything's fine."

"Okay, Azron and Xharon have brought some rope. We're going to lower it down to you."

"Okay," Handen called, but he was suddenly doubtful that he would be able to leave this place, whether the arcane magnetism of the pool would let him leave. But he had to. It was not time for him to die yet. He still had a mission to complete.

He unfastened his small waterskin from his hip and emptied the contents onto the ground, then lowered the container into the pool. Some of the liquid touched his hand and tingled there uneasily. He had a sudden thought that, had he not been immortal, the very touch of the fountain of death would have killed him.

With the waterskin full, the nagging coaxing sensation of the pool seemed to lessen. Handen found he was able to walk away, back to the cave's entrance, without a struggle. As long as he carried a piece of the fountain, he knew, he would cease to be the cave's prisoner.

He looked at the lowered rope as if seeing it for the first time. It did not belong here, he felt. There was never supposed to be a way out of the death cave. Then he looked up at the faces of his friends, back up at a world where sunlight and clear skies were merely a few minutes' walk away. Suddenly Handen felt as he had when he had first escaped from the Bin—a frenzied combination of relief and freedom. He climbed the rope, leaving the deadly yet strangely seductive solitude of the death cave behind him.

12

Hot Pursuit

There have been countless poems and songs ode to Dawncastle by morning, whole overtures dedicated to Bersch's most resplendent and remarkable building, a thousand artists who have snapped their brushes in frustration trying to capture its ethereal magnificence. It stands aloft at the center of the industrially environed city of Argustin, reflecting the gradual colorings of dawn throughout the prisms of its glass and polished steel architecture, appearing like a conjurer's crystal against the smoky city skies.

By ingenious design, the great palace magnified and reflected the light of the day, twisting and bending the rays of the sun so that they spread and shone in a smoldering, nearly opaque glow. In the hushed moments before dawn, the building would be the first thing to light up the morning sky, turning a pale blue as it intercepted the earliest hints of the coming daylight. Then suddenly, brilliantly, it would cycle through a multitude of burning hues as the sun began to rise, pulsing spears of red, orange, and gold as quick and random as a midnight bonfire.

The tower shape of the Dawncastle, a maelstrom of multifarious spires and archways tapering and entwining to a needle point, meant the construct appeared like a brilliant teardrop of fire by mid morning, shining so brightly that it could be seen for miles around. The surrounding city, though built high and impressive itself, was entirely outshone by the crystalline tower, like a weak, ailing king under a still-marvelous crown.

For those who lived inside Dawncastle, the effects of a clear-skied dawn were just as remarkable as those seen from the outside. Having spent the night cooling gradually under the stars, the cold corridors of the palace would become suddenly and welcomingly warm, washing the panorama of the surrounding city in a rosy glow. Windows formerly paneled by the dark of night into a hard, lifeless onyx were reborn as salmon-tinted crystal.

The steel bones and window skin of the tremendous tower absorbed and radiated everything that was wondrous about the new life of morning.

Which was fine. If you were a morning person.

Emperor Tomberry Torrid Draegul the Tenth was not a morning person. Emperor Draegul got up when he damn well felt like it, and woe betide anyone who interrupted his sleeping patterns. He had once ordered the execution of every bird in a two-mile radius simply because of an over-enthusiastic dawn chorus. He was not a man best caught in a bad mood.

Today he rose at roughly noon. At his first stirrings, the harp player positioned discreetly in the corner of the room began to pluck a slow and soothing tune. Predictably the musician was promptly struck unconscious by the brick Draegul kept at his bedside specifi-cally for throwing at staff. This happened every time the Emperor awoke, but the musician would gladly take a half-hearted brick to the head each day rather than face the consequences of absenteeism. The player and his instrument were dragged quietly away by the ultra-discreet Whimstaff.

Emperor Draegul smacked his lips. "Maggot?" he called.

A tall elderly figure dressed in white robes appeared almost magi-cally by Draegul's side. His name was not Maggot, but Draegul rarely bothered with the names of his attendant staff and called people whatever he felt like.

"I'm in a blue mood today, Maggot. And I think I want a rhinoceros risotto for breakfast."

"As you wish, Your Incredibleness," said Maggot. Maggot was head of the Whimstaff—those responsible for making sure Draegul's every whim and desire were met to the closest degree of immediacy. It was a demanding and stressful job, and position of Head of Whimstaff was notoriously short-lived. Maggot, however, had survived for a record three years by being ready for anything and being able to partially anticipate the vastly unpredictable moods of his master.

He already had his staff on standby with the tinted blinds and curtains that would change the interior color of Dawncastle to whatever suited Draegul's current mood. The rhinoceros breakfast was a more complicated task, seeing as the nearest rhinoceros was likely several hundred miles away in the Southwestern savannah regions.

Oh, well. Maggot would do what he usually did when the Emperor had a hankering for a rare or non-existent food—mash up some chicken into a pâté and cut it into an interesting shape. With any luck, Draegul wouldn't even notice—Maggot was quite sure the Emperor only asked for such unusual breakfasts to test his limitations anyway. However, if Draegul did notice that the meat in his rhinoceros risotto was merely re-formed chicken, Maggot would more than likely face a horrible execution.

Maggot's was a hard life, and he sighed heavily once he was safely out of his master's earshot.

Back in the master bedroom, Draegul emerged from his bed. The Whimstaff, operating with their expert discretion, had begun warming the room a few hours before the Emperor's estimated time of awakening, so Draegul felt no morning chill as he strode toward his dressing table. He arrived and looked in the mirror.

"Casual," he muttered.

Immediately, five maids appeared from various hidden doorways, each with an item of clothing. In the blink of an eye, Draegul was dressed by his dexterous attendants in a comfortable pair of jodhpurs and riding boots, complemented nicely by a black silken shirt that was frilled only slightly effeminately at the sleeves. Draegul gazed critically in the mirror and smiled a satisfied smile. It was easy to look good when you were rich beyond the dreams of even the greediest merchant.

He held his arms out while he was adorned with the thin, silver crown and the ceremonial weapons that he was rarely seen without. He tested the mechanism of his rifle and studied the edge of his sword. A satisfied smile once again made a delicate crease in his features. He was ready for the day.

Draegul's schedule was an undemanding one. He had most of the day booked off for surprising Maggot with impossible whims, a pastime he found most amusing. Later, he might spar with one of his elite, just to keep his sword skills as finely honed as the blade he carried. After that, he imagined, there would be servants to torment, peasants to terrify, and an army of concubines to take advantage of. But for now, he would spend the morning as he spent every morning —walking around Dawncastle looking for reasons to execute people.

The Emperor emerged into the freshly blue-tinted corridors of the upper chambers. Through the surrounding windows, he could see the city of Argustin stretched before him. Not much impressed Draegul, but the cityscape of Argustin always filled him with something akin to pride. He watched as airschooners drifted between towers and archways of steel and stone, and as railcars sped smoothly across the elevated railings, their propellers burring over the tower tops and domed roofs. In the distance, a cloud of brown-tinted smoke billowed softly from a thousand chimneys, flavoring the skies of the factory quarter with the acrid smell of progress.

As he gazed across the high-topped buildings of the capital, his thoughts turned to the two escaped doomsayers. He had been thinking more and more about them lately and wondered if Blungkit had been successful in their capture. More, he thought about the message the fugitives were carrying...the destruction of the planet by some intruding astral body. A bleak prospect. Draegul briefly envisioned his city burning beneath cosmic flames, his citizens dying screaming in an alien heat. It was not an image he found wholly unattractive, but the prospect annoyed him greatly. If anyone was going to lay waste to the world, he felt, it was going to be Emperor Tomberry Torrid Draegul the Tenth.

A familiar whispering sensation sounded in his ear as he stared with his mind's eye. One of these days, he knew, he would have to see a doctor about the gentle yet incessant chittering noise that came to him whenever he tried to think. He found his thoughts turned yet again to the desert project—Operation Deadwaker, as the project managers had come to call it. He reminded himself to check on the progress of the archaeologists and engineers. Time was short, and he was beginning to think he'd have to start executing people to re-motivate the work force.

He could not afford to have a lackluster crew working on Operation Deadwaker. The fate of the world might depend on it.

THE WAGON TRUNDLED across the Dozantyne Shrub, the rotting forest lessening to a moribund smear of geography behind them. The doomsayers rolled along at the pace they had become accustomed to, though their traveling arrangements were a little different than usual this time. Before setting off that day, Handen had asked Xharon if he could ride ahead on Prancer. Xharon had agreed without protest—the request was one of the few things the former Hostilities Advisor had said since returning from the fountain of death. So now he rode ahead, silent and alone.

At the moment, Bip was finding it hard to feel sorry for the immortal. He was concerned with Handen's obvious self-isolation, but the upshot was that he was able to sit next to Xharon on the wagon—and had deliberately missed his turn at rest so he could do so. In the back of the wagon, Azron was using his unexpected downtime to get some extra sleep, while in the front, Bip's hormone-addled brain sought desperately for something to say.

It wasn't that Bip hadn't any experience in talking to girls. He had talked to plenty of girls. It was just that none of them had been as immediately half-naked as Xharon. Nor was it a question of self-confidence; months of hard travel had done a lot of good for Bip's physical appearance. His weedy frame had worked into something more sinewy, and the long days of sunlight had turned his near-gray complexion a healthy brown and his washy, almost-blond hair into a robust gold. In short, Bip—underneath the travel-dirt, torn clothes, and scratched glasses—was looking better than ever. But still he couldn't think of a word to say to this girl.

Eventually, after what seemed like a warm eternity of silence, Xharon spoke up. "He's an awfully somber chap, isn't he?" she said.

"Whu?" replied Bip, who was so busy thinking of something to say that he had temporarily forgotten how to speak.

"Handen," said Xharon, nodding to the solitary figure on horseback. "A very serious man."

Bip cleared his throat, glad of the chance for conversation. "He's okay most of the time. He just gets a little gloomy now and then. Mostly when he's bored."

Xharon squinted thoughtfully at Handen's back. "I would've thought that being immortal would be brilliant. The things he must have seen, the places he must have been!"

"Well, that's the problem, really," said Bip. "He was locked up for hundreds of years, and he can't remember most of the places he's been, and all of the people he's met are dead, and all of the things he's done don't matter to anyone anymore."

"I see," said Xharon, though she didn't appear to be paying much attention. "Do you think he has a girlfriend?" she said unexpectedly.

Bip tried hard to keep his mental footing at this unexpected rock in the stream of conversation. "I doubt it," he said. "I should imagine any relationship he formed in the lunatic asylum was less than serious."

"Oh," said Xharon, and went back to staring at Handen.

Bip thought desperately of a way to steer the discussion back to more immediate interests. "So you're the princess," he ventured flatly.

Xharon gave him a look somewhere between contempt and pity. "That's right," she said.

"So I expect one day you'll be the queen or something?"

"Oh no. Never. They'd never let a woman be Emperor...or Empress, I suppose. Only uncle Tommy's sons are heirs to the throne."

"Really? And what are they like?"

"No one knows." Xharon shrugged. "Their identities are kept a great secret—for their own protection, of course."

"But they're your cousins," Bip said, frowning. "You must have seen them at least once?"

Xharon shook her head. "From the day that they are born, they are hidden from society, raised and educated in secret. No one but Draegul's most trusted advisors ever see his children."

"Bizarre," concluded Bip. The wagon trundled along in silence for a while before he spoke again. "Surely your auntie must tell you about them?"

Xharon said nothing.

Bip continued. "I mean, she must see them now and again, being their mother and all."

"My auntie is dead," Xharon said.

Bip blushed and looked at his feet. "I'm sorry," he said.

"You needn't be," Xharon replied dismissively. "It happened a long time ago. She died of an illness—she had a weak heart, you see. The doctors said there was nothing they could do."

The Kaneqian scanned the horizon, thinking of something sensitive yet tactful to say.

"It hurt my father the most, I think," Xharon continued. "Uncle Tommy called a week of mourning throughout the Empire's heart, of course. Though he never seemed very broken up about it—always too wrapped up in his projects. But my father...my father was very close to her, and it nearly ended him when she died." Xharon furrowed her brow, peering into a memory. "She was very beautiful. She smiled a lot, I remember. I think that's why Uncle Tommy married her, really, why he made my father a duke. She really was very pretty."

"It must run in the family," said Bip, then immediately wished he hadn't. For the second time in a short while, he blushed furiously.

Xharon looked at him and smiled. "People do say I have her eyes."

Bip frowned and blinked owlishly. "What…did she leave them to you in her will or something?"

Xharon stared hard at the Kaneqian with a familiar expression of contempt and pity.

"I think I'll swap places with Azron, now, if you don't mind," she said.

"Of course not," said Bip, and once again cursed his inherent lack of debonair.

THEY TRAVELED for two more days, brushing through the landscape stolidly and with little pause. They sensed the vague feeling of leaving nowhere behind in favor of somewhere and that the journey of days, months, and millennia was finally coming to its last furlong. Unfortunately, they didn't sense the presence of the Regulators behind them, drawing closer and closer as the miles went by.

HANDEN SAT IN SILENCE, as he had for the last few days, his hunter's eyes searching through a far and away void, his fighter's hands twiddling distractedly with the waterskin before him.

They had made healthy progress since the dead wood, traveling many miles and at last nearing the end of the Dozantyne Shrub. Now the incessant, flawless horizons had yielded to squat stony hillocks, which, in turn, yielded to larger, rocky hills. These hills, Xharon had said, would eventually spiral away into the Oaken Mons, a great winding whip of green peaks that separated the Empire's heart from the western provinces. Traveling along the southern borders as they were, the fugitives would be able to pass the mountain range without resorting to the heavily patrolled byways or airboat services.

Though Argustin was still far away, the doomsayers were drawing comfortably close. That was why, placated by their own sense of optimism, the travelers had taken a break from their rigid schedule to rest the horses and eat a hot lunch in the middle of the afternoon, rather than waiting for supper that night.

They sat atop one of the larger hills watching the level expanse of the Shrub stretch away behind them, seeming still and carpet-like in the far distance. Azron lay on his back, relaxing and blowing cigarette smoke into the air above him while Bip tended to the cooking. Xharon sharpened her axes on a whetstone, singing quietly in her faltering soprano. Everyone seemed content bar Handen, who slouched in the same hunch of moody contemplation he had adopted since filling his waterskin at the fountain of death. He stared down at the elixir that would provide a final and ultimate cure to his immortality.

He should have felt happier, he knew, having finally found the one thing he had hoped to find since the discovery of his ageless invulnerability, but he could not help feeling strangely glum. He had a job to do before he could end his life, a mission to fulfill and a promise to keep to all those he had cared about...all those who were now so much dust in the wind, long dead and sketchy in memory.

On some mornings, after the plaguing dreams of the half-remembered lifetimes he had left in his wake like the shed skins of a reptile, the compulsion to drink the thick, brown water and damn the consequences was unbearable. Presently, he found himself barely suppressing the urge to dip a finger into the mouth of the waterskin and lick the result, just to see what would happen.

His gloom was twofold. Part of him couldn't wait to drink the water and end a lifetime of too many years to bear, but part of him was scared also of what might come afterward, and whether the faces of countless foes long since dispatched would be waiting for him in the dark.

He wondered if, when the time came, he would really be able to drink from the fountain of death. The urge to leave the world was strong, for Handen had grown tired of it a thousand times over, but he felt he might hesitate, as one might hesitate to leave a boring party or put down a bad book, just in case he were to miss out on something interesting.

Handen sighed. In his hand, he had hoped he had found the ultimate solution. He should have known from the deep well of his experience that nothing in life was so straightforward.

Bip looked up from his cooking over the flames of the daytime campfire and once again observed the melancholic fatigue swamping his companion. He was worried about Handen. He had come to regard the first volunteer not just as a valuable ally but also as a good and trusted friend. He envied him in many ways and wondered how far in his quest he would have come without the stark professionalism of the adventurer. He grew worried at these signs of weakness in the usually stoic man and did not like the way that, when at rest, he would withdraw from the world, contemplative and distant. Handen's moods had not improved with the discovery of the fountain of death —for which he had quested for over several centuries—but, instead, had worsened.

In the background, Bip was dimly aware that Xharon had stopped the meticulous working of her axe blades and now stood to perform the frenzied but nonetheless impressive kata she practiced every night. Bip turned to watch as the young princess swung her axes in quick blurring arcs, sometimes allowing the momentum of her body to spin a leg out in a high whirling kick or bend her torso in a spiraling side-flip. Now and then she would let out high-pitched yelps of aggression, like an abbreviated version of her war cry. Bip watched the display with great interest, although for baser reasons than the appreciation of finely executed martial arts.

After a while, it became apparent that Handen, too, had become fixated on the display.

"Good, isn't she?" he said.

Bip started at the sound of his friend's comment. Handen had spent so much time in silence since the incident in the dead wood that his voice had taken on a scratchy and unfamiliar tone. He turned to look at the adventurer and was pleased to see that a sense of connection had returned to Handen's eyes. The former hopeless melancholy had been banished for a time, replaced by a more familiar expression of calculating interest. Bip winced as he felt a twang of jealousy in the pit of his stomach.

"I mean, she's a little showy, and her economy of movement isn't ideal, but there's definite flair. A natural balance and poise. She could be quite the fighter, given the chance."

Bip nodded his agreement, though had no real opinion on the matter. Even with his occasional sparring matches with Handen, he still hadn't managed to develop much of a knack for hand-to-hand combat.

"The axes are definitely a bad choice of weapon, though," continued Handen.

"She'd be better off with a nice short sword and a lightweight shield—something more suited to her body shape."

Bip looked at the warrior princess, twirling the stunted-looking axes with frightening abandon.

"I don't know," he ventured. "She seems to be doing all right to me."

Handen gave a lazy half-shrug, as though not really hearing what the Kaneqian was saying. Bip looked at his friend closely and noticed that Handen's stolid and calculating gaze was a little warmer than usual; something in his shell of stoicism seemed to tilt affectionately.

They turned back to Xharon's kata, both men marveling at different sides of the same shape. Likely they could have sat there watching for a long while if the ground behind them had not suddenly exploded.

BLUNGKIT RODE at the head of his exhausted but still determined party. Of the fifty men he had originally set out with, only thirty remained—lank and despondent in their sweat-stained uniforms. Many of the others had fallen to heatstroke or exhaustion, victims of the posse's ruthless and unforgiving traveling pace. More still had lost their mounts to the inhospitable terrain. All these men had been left behind at various stages of their journey, sacrificed to the greater good or, more accurately, to Blungkit's agenda.

The Pin Constable had cursed his luck when arriving at the Bone Desert outpost. The available reinforcements had consisted of greenhorns and strays, those Regulators who were deemed too inexperienced or too incompetent to be placed in more active regions, and thus were made soft and weak from lack of challenge. Blungkit was sure that, had he set off with a contingent of Panthalus men, fifty Regulators would be standing with him now instead of thirty. Still, the important thing was that he had caught up with his quarry. The fugitives were within his grasp.

He grinned carnivorously as he lowered the telescope from his eye. He could clearly see the camp, finally see the faces of the prisoners who had made a fool of him all those months ago. And, incredibly, they hadn't been detected. For some reason or other, the fugitives had not seen the approach of Blungkit's posse, even though they had made no real attempt at stealth.

Still smiling, he folded the telescope and handed it to his lieutenant, a young P.C. by the name of Darby, within whom he had discovered a dogged nastiness that he recognized as true to his own heart.

"Got 'em by the curlies now, Darby," he said.

"Do we approach?" replied his protégé.

"Nah," said Blungkit, "there's an old saying, Darby my lad: why risk a scratching when you can kill a cat with a half-brick and not even get out of your chair?"

Darby frowned. It was not a saying he had heard before, though he could see the truth in it.

Blungkit turned to the beast wranglers, the men in charge of the huge, long-necked and horn-headed uberbeasts. Thankfully all three of the beasts they had set out with were still holding well, one used as a packhorse for food and supplies, and the other two bearing massive assault cannons harnessed to their flanks.

"Right," said Blungkit. "Let's give these buggers something to think about." He raised his fist above his head. "Fire!"

The wranglers shouted the command words to their charges, and the beasts braced themselves, moaning their low, dumb bellows in worried anticipation. Then the gunners, riding atop the monstrous gun bearers, set the fuse on the cannons. The twin guns boomed apocalyptically as they sent their heavy iron cannonballs flying in search of targets. Blungkit grinned at the low, threatening whistle made in their wake.

<hr>

HANDEN WAS FIRST on his feet, the dreamy fascination erased from his features as quickly as snow melting in fire. Bip was up a second later, his face a comic epitome of shock. Xharon had frozen in her kata, narrowly avoiding the blades of her own axes as she ground suddenly to a halt.

The three looked around for signs of threat; the air hung with the unique stillness that only appears after moments of the sudden and dangerous. It wasn't until they heard Azron that they realized what had happened.

"Eeeeeeeep?" said a voice barely recognizable as belonging to the Port Town man.

Where the thief had been lying down, he now sat bolt upright, his face caked with dust and his cigarette blackened and twisted. His eyes were stupendously wide, and his confident grin had been replaced by a slack-jawed grimace of horrified surprise. He once again gave off the low keening sound that seemed to escape from his throat of its own accord.

"Eeeeeeeep?"

At his feet a crater, four feet wide, coned down to a small but lethal-looking cannonball that gleamed dully in the late-morning light, steaming with quiet relief. Had the ball landed slightly to the left, Azron would have been relieved of his legs.

"Hit the deck!" shouted Handen, and everyone, including Bip, who wasn't sure what the deck was or why they should hit it, fell to their bellies.

"Great holy bastards!" exclaimed Azron, crawling over to his comrades. "What in the backside of hell was that all about?"

"Over here!" said Handen and began crawling toward a large and sturdy-looking boulder. Eventually, when all four of them were huddled against the rock, Handen pointed out the obvious. "We're under fire," he said. "Cannon fire." He took in Bip's blank expression. "Like a pistola but much, much bigger."

Bip swallowed. He had thought the idea of the flintlocks a little nightmarish. To imagine one of a larger scale was terrible to behold.

"I say!" Xharon said, glancing at each of her comrades in turn. "Isn't this exciting?"

"No!" Azron replied hotly. "It bloody well isn't! I damn well nearly lost my knees! I like my knees! They're handy for all sorts of things!"

"Where are they firing from?" interrupted Bip.

"Good question," replied Handen. Bip once again perceived how the adventurer only truly seemed to be alive—to be there—when there was conflict at hand.

Handen began to raise his head slowly above the rock. The others followed cautiously. As they peered over the boulder, the unruffled terrain of the Shrub once again opened before them, though now the flat horizon was marred by a group of Regulators, huddled together like a sudden gray pimple. They seemed impossibly far away to be such an immediate threat, but a threat they were.

"Damn," said Handen. "They've caught up with us."

"Regulators," breathed Bip, a faint finger of terror gliding up his spine.

"What's that with them?" said Azron, pointing to the larger mounds standing with their hunters.

"Uberbeasts," Handen said, squinting slightly into the distance. He recognized them well, and dimly remembered having to fight one once, long ago. "It's how they're transporting the cannons."

Xharon looked affronted. "You mean to tell me they're making those poor animals carry heavy machinery in this heat? That's horrible!"

Azron and Handen exchanged a cynical glance. "Yes," said Azron. "Truly horrible. Why don't you go and give them a telling-off, yeah?"

Before anyone could stop her, Xharon was on her feet. "You know, I just might," she said.

"Are you mental, girl? They'll blow you to smithereens!" said the thief.

"Of course they won't," said Xharon, haughtily. "I am their princess, after all."

Handen rolled his eyes. "We may know that you're their princess, Xharon, but all they see is a speck on the horizon aiding and abetting some other specks on the horizon. If you try and go over there, they'll fire on you for sure."

"Don't be silly," said Xharon.

For a moment, Bip was terrified that she really was going to try and approach the Regulators, but then, far in the distance, there was a small, almost insignificant flash from where the uberbeasts were standing. A second later, the flash was followed by a loud boom that echoed through the Shrub like a death knell. This boom was followed by a dread and promising whistling noise.

"Scatter!" roared Handen.

The companions did not need to be told twice. They leapt in opposite directions as the boulder that had given them the illusion of safety suddenly burst into tiny pieces of shrapnel. Bip sat up where he had landed, raising a shaky hand to a cut on his cheek. He stared dumbfounded at the rubble of their former shelter.

That could have been you, said a smug little voice in the back of his head.

Handen was on his feet before the dust began to settle, pulling Bip up by the scruff of his shirt. "To the wagon!" he shouted, though to Bip's blasted ears, his voice seemed curiously far away. The fugitives started to head toward where they had left the wagon but stopped abruptly in their tracks. Where the wagon had been, there now lay a pile of wooden rubble. A broken wheel spun sadly to rest.

"They blew up the bloody wagon!" Azron shouted indignantly. "All of our stuff was in there!"

"To the horses!" shouted Handen, and this time when they got there, they were relieved to find their mounts in one piece, though somewhat jittery from the sudden chaos. Without delay, Xharon leapt gracefully onto Prancer, the heavily muscled charger remaining admirably calm in the surrounding panic. Bip, though, disorientated from the ordeal, managed to saddle up one of the wagon horses only after a frustrating and frantic dance, made all the more difficult by the occasional cannonballs that would rain down with whistling fury, throwing up clouds of dirt and dust with powerful abandon. By the time Bip had struggled into his saddle, Azron and Handen were already mounted and ready to leave.

"Move out!" bellowed Handen, and once again, even in the midst of pandemonium, Bip observed how natural and at ease the immortal seemed when the world was erupting around him.

Wagon-less and leaving most of their supplies behind, the fugitives galloped away in the direction of Argustin, devil clouds of dust settling behind them.

"CEASE FIRE!" roared Blungkit, and the gunners halted the clockwork process of stoking, loading, and firing. The uberbeasts relaxed as the echo of gunfire faded to nothingness. Blungkit grinned his wet, wooden grin.

"Should we prepare for pursuit, sir?" said Darby.

"No rush, lad," said Blungkit. "We've got 'em where we want 'em—scared and disorientated. It's just a matter of running 'em into the ground now. And then..." Blungkit patted the grip of his flintlock pistola, a newer model to replace the one Handen had stolen. "And then the fun begins," he finished, and gave a guttural and menacing laugh. Darby, eager to show solidarity with his new leader, began to join in with his own menacing laugh. Blungkit turned to him with a look of disgust on his face.

"What are you laughing at?" he said.

Darby's pockmarked face went blank. "I don't know," he muttered.

"Well don't," said Blungkit. "You sound like an idiot."

Darby's brow furrowed in confusion. He made as if to say something, then, wisely, thought better of it. One day he hoped to have underlings of his own to boss around, and he understood, on a socially philosophical level, that a certain amount of abuse had to be tolerated before you could rightly dish it out to others.

Blungkit scanned the horizon, that same predatory grin twisting his already unpleasant face into something near demonic. He began laughing quietly to himself again. This time Darby left him to it.

* * *

HIGH ABOVE THE trailing smoke of the cannons, swaying in the breezes of the open sky, Mr. Random looked down at the pack of Regulators, appearing like gray-coated ants from his vantage point.

He bridged his long fingers and smiled to himself. He enjoyed human nature, he really did. Just when you thought the world was full of useless, ineffectual weaklings, it turned up a card like Blungkit—a man more rabid wolf than law enforcer.

He was optimistic that Blungkit would catch up with the troublemakers and, with a little encouragement, butcher them mercilessly and without hesitation. It was good to know, very reassuring, that the few people on the planet who could stand in the way of his plans would soon be murdered by the supposed peacekeepers of their own civilization. But a smidgen of doubt still lurked awkwardly at the back of his mind. What if Blungkit, despite his advantages, was to fail for any reason?

As any respectable being of concentrated nastiness knew, the odds could never be too favorable, and overkill was better than no kill at all. What was needed was a little extra dilemma...

Bobbing gently in the air currents around him, Mr. Random grinned to himself. He snapped his fingers and disappeared.

There was always mischief in the world for those who knew how to make it.

BIP CLUNG tightly to the neck of his horse, gritting his teeth as the momentum of the gallop shook and shuddered him madly like a pea in a rattle. He had not been able to saddle his mount properly in all the confusion and, foolishly, had dropped his reins when they had first fled from the wrath of the Regulators. Now he clung desperately to his panicked horse and hoped dearly that the beast would instinctively follow its companions and not flee in a direction of its own choosing.

In front of him, he could see Azron having a hard time on the uncomfortable saddle as he clung to Handen's waist, and Xharon and Prancer maintaining a breakneck gallop in the far distance.

Above all of the noise and confusion, Bip could hear the pounding of his heart beating hard enough to make his vision swim with each percussion. Though the steady tension of being a fugitive was by no means an un-stressful experience, this mad dash had brought Bip as close to utter panic as he had been since his flight from the yeti. He was beginning to think that he might black out, then almost certainly he would be thrown beneath the hooves of his own horse.

The next long minutes of flight were tooth-grindingly tense for Bip, who thought that at any minute his saddle might slide farther down his horse's flank, or that the Regulators might suddenly appear behind them, whooping and closing in for the kill.

Following Xharon's lead, they rode farther into hills, crisscrossing beneath miniature cliff faces and descending into deep, sudden valleys. As they rode on, the hills and cliffs became tighter, and pockets of forest obscured the afternoon sunlight. Soon they were traveling through what appeared to be a labyrinthine system of tunnels and gullies.

As they approached a fork in the pathway, Handen yelled for them to halt.

Thankfully, Bip's mount came to a stop of its own accord, and the Kaneqian gasped with sudden relief. He quickly retrieved his mount's reins and adjusted the saddle as best he could.

"Why have we stopped?" he said between breaths.

Handen turned to him. "We're going to have to split up. "

"What?!"

"He's right, mate," said Azron, who was breathing hard himself. "Those buggers back there are running us into the ground—if we don't do something to slow 'em down we're dead meat."

"We don't have time to try to cover our tracks," continued Handen. "Our only hope is to split up and rendezvous later on. That way we can confuse the Regulators, or at the very least divide their forces."

Bip looked at the determined expressions of his friends. "I don't like it…" he muttered.

"I know, kid," said Handen. "I don't like it either, but it's the only way. "

"What's the plan?" said Xharon, her eyes burning eagerly.

"Azron and I will take the left path," said Handen. "You and Bip will take the right."

Xharon looked less than impressed with her lot but nodded anyway. Bip felt a sudden wince of sorrow behind his eyes. He did not want to be so suddenly split from the people he had grown to trust so much.

Handen turned his horse around, preparing to depart. "If everything goes okay, we'll either meet at Argustin or on the way. If not…" Handen looked at his companions each in turn. "Don't wait up and don't look back. We have a message to deliver and a world to save. Don't forget why we're here in the first place. Good luck."

With that, Handen spurred his horse into a gallop. He and Azron rode away, leaving only dust and silence in their wake.

The two remaining travelers waited for a while, watching them leave. Eventually Xharon turned in her saddle toward to Bip.

"Think you can keep up?" she said, cracking a wry smile that suddenly made the Kaneqian feel a little better about things.

"I can try," replied Bip.

"Then let's ride!"

SOMETIME LATER, the Regulators arrived at the fork in the path. Blungkit held up a hand, and the procession behind him came to an ordered halt. He looked at the two sets of tracks and smiled to himself. He knew that this was more than likely a hasty attempt by his quarry to evade complete capture—or possibly a studied move to divide his forces. However, Blungkit could not see how dividing his forces would help the fugitives in any way. After all, fifteen on two were just as unfavorable odds as thirty on four.

Darby rode up behind the Pin Constable. "What now, sir?" he said.

"We split up," Blungkit said promptly. "You take twelve men and go right, and I'll take twelve men and go left. We'll leave the uberbeasts and a few handlers here—speed is now essential." Blungkit turned so he could address his entire force. "All right, men, this is where it ends. They are divided and ripe for conquering. They are scared, and they are few. Ride the bastards down and show no mercy!"

A roar of approval came from the Regulators, like the baying of hounds on a hunt. After so many miles of travel, the moment of victory was finally within their grasp.

The two contingents split and thundered down their respective pathways. Blungkit, riding at the head of his division, grinned like a hyena with the smell of fresh meat in its nose.

BIP AND XHARON rode hard but were forced to slow when the ground beneath them became stony and unpredictable. Prancer had already had a few narrow encounters with rocks jutting suddenly from the long grass, and the cliffs to either side of the path would occasionally dislodge miniature avalanches of smaller stones that, while not a great danger to the mounts, were certainly an inconvenience.

They rode slowly through the eerily quiet valley-cum-canyon, safe in the knowledge that anybody pursuing them would also have to slow their pace. Without realizing it, Bip began to whistle nervously through his teeth. Xharon turned and made a shushing motion. Up ahead there was a sound like a deep thud, as though something heavy had just fallen from a tree. Bip halted abruptly, pulling on the reins of his horse. He held his breath as he listened. For a while, there was only the sound of a few insects buzzing lazily in the long grass. Then, suddenly and disturbingly, there was another thump. This time Bip was certain he could feel the ground vibrate slightly.

Xharon turned around in her saddle again. "What was that?" she mouthed.

Bip shrugged just as another thump shook the ground around them.

Almost instantaneously the two riders dismounted, Xharon drawing her twin axes with a flourish and Bip clutching the hilt of Brian. Bip held his breath, staring hard at the pathway before him. A slight bulge in one of the cliff walls and several tall trees obscured the view of the pathway ahead. Another thump resounded, closer this time, and Bip was certain that whatever was responsible for the noises was approaching directly in front of them.

Without warning, a deer burst from the bushes and sprinted toward them. Bip almost choked as his heart leapt into his throat. He stumbled and fell backward as the animal hurried its way past them. The Kaneqian nearly laughed with relief.

"It was a deer!" he said. "Here was me thinking that we were about to be confronted by some huge and terrible monster, and it was just a deer! What do you think about that, Xharon?" Bip got to his feet, still chuckling to himself. "I said, 'What do you think about that, Xharon?'" he repeated. Hearing no reply, Bip turned to his companion.

"Xharon?"

The warrior princess stood with her axes slack in her hands, her body limp, and the color drained from her skin. Her head tilted backward as though she had fallen asleep on her feet.

"Xharon?" Bip stood by the princess and followed her gaze upward. And then upward again. "Oh," he said. "Oh, crap."

Towering above them, with a smile that was successful in connoting a number of unpleasant things, leaning casually on a club that was nothing more than a branchless tree, stood a giant.

"Fe Fi Fo Fum…" it said, in a voice that seemed to reverberate like a rockslide. "Ah smell something am gonna eet!"

Not for the first time that day, Bip found himself on the verge of blacking out.

HANDEN WAITED, crouched at his vantage point overlooking the slim, overgrown canyon floor below him. He was confident that even though Azron had left a trail a blind man could follow with ease, anyone crossing this part of the path would slow down sufficiently for his purposes. Hidden on the tree-laden top of the muddy cliff, Handen waited in ambush.

When the Regulators had caught up with them, he had been put in mind of the hunting habits of a creature he had once read about called a stoat. The creature was vicious, but slower than its prey of choice, the rabbit. However, the stoat was a relentless hunter and infallible tracker and though the rabbit might run for miles upon end, eventually—when it thought it was safe—there would be the stoat, approaching with casual doom.

Handen was determined not to become the rabbit. Not to run himself into exhaustion and be consumed by a large and merciless hunter. The old Hostilities Advisor adage came to mind: when caught in a deadly game of cat and mouse, don't be the mouse.

The adventurer shifted his position slightly, distributing his weight evenly. If all went according to plan, then any Regulator force following the single horse tracks he had left would be expecting no fight—only pursuit and capture. He intended to confound their expectations in the most violent way possible.

Getting Xharon and Bip out of the way had been the hard part, and the fork in the road had certainly proved a blessing. He knew that the younger companions would have doubtless tried to aid him in his ambush and, though fifteen-to-one odds were a gaunt feasibility even for an immortal, the chances of two people as inexperienced in battle as Bip and Xharon getting hurt or killed were very high indeed. He'd had no such anxiety when deciding to bring Azron with him—the thief's talent for self-preservation would keep him at a safe distance from the action and give him a good head start if the ambush failed.

With any luck, the attack would slow the Regulators down enough that they could make their escape. And if the worst were to happen and he was captured, he might still buy his friends some time to reach Argustin.

Handen checked his weapons. It took some time. Then he waited.

GIANTKIN WERE NOT common in the lowlands of Bersch, normally residing on mountaintops where the air was thin and conditions harsh. Indeed, it was these conditions that had caused the giant race to evolve as large as they were, growing anything up to thirty feet tall. Even so, some giantkin tribes managed to find their way to lower lands, where they were generally avoided by their neighbors and, despite a typically volatile and bully-ish temperament, were happy to be left to their own devices.

However, even in the tribes of a race famed for their nasty person-alities, renegades were born, those giants who were so stupidly cruel or hostile that they couldn't function within their respective commu-nities. These giants would eventually be banished and forced to wander the lower lands on their own, foraging and surviving by terrorizing the races that were smaller than them…which was pretty much all of the races.

Bregus was one of these renegades. An unusually short giant, at a mere twenty-three-feet tall, Bregus had always carried a lot of ingrown hostility toward the world and had eventually been banished from his tribe for eating his baby brother for no apparent reason other than that he had been in a bad mood. There were few giantkin left in the continent of Regalious and even fewer renegades, since even a giant was not immune to the heavy artillery of the Empire. Bregus had survived by laying low in the southlands, making sure that he attacked only small packs of travelers and left no evidence of his feasting.

Like all giants, Bregus was fiercely protective of his territory. He stared down over his ample gut at the tiny intruders, scratching his massive, hairless head with one of the stubby fingers at the end of an overly long arm. As per usual in a confrontational situation, he grumbled the ancient threat-song that giantkin had passed down since the dawn of their history.

"I'll grind yer bones to make me bread!" he boomed.

Despite his terror, Bip couldn't help but frown.

"What do you mean?" he said. "You can't make bread from bones. You need yeast and things, don't you? Or flour?"

Xharon stepped back until she was level with the Kaneqian. "I think he means he'll grind our bones in order to fashion them into tools used in the making of bread..."

"Oh," said Bip.

Bregus, who had never really understood the threat-song himself, listened to the exchange with a puzzled expression before attempting to continue the rhyme. "Aye, that's right... Fashion tools to make me bread...and...erm... Fe Fi Fo Fum!"

"You said that bit already," said Bip. His sheer terror had seemed to temporarily disconnect his mouth from his brain.

"Aye, ah know!" roared the giant. "Shut yer mooth, ya wee erseface, am trying ta think!" He stamped a foot on the ground in irritation, the shockwave of which threw the companions to the ground. Bip, knees trembling, decided to bite his traitor tongue.

The giant put a finger to its chin. "Now... Fe Fi Fo Fum, ah smell the blood of...someone...and even if he's dead...ah'll fashion him into kitchen...utensils..."

He stared hard into space. "I'm sure that's not right."

Bip, sensing an opportunity, began edging back toward his horse. "Well, that's all right, I'm sure it will come to you eventually," he said.

Xharon began to follow Bip's example. "Yes, we'll come back later if you like..."

"Hold on a wee minute!" Bregus roared. "Where dez you think yous are going? Am not finished with yous yet!"

Bip and Xharon froze in their tracks.

"Now," began the giant, bending down until his enormous face loomed almost directly over the prone companions. "Ah've caught you trespassing on my territory, yes?"

Bip and Xharon nodded their heads in unison, dumb with fear. "So," continued the giant, "whut kind of giant would ah be if a lets ye get away withoot being eaten?"

Bip gulped hard. "A big, friendly one?" he ventured.

"Aye!" growled Bregus. "And we all knows whut happens to them!"

Bip and Xharon shook their heads in unison.

"They git their erses kicked by the other giants, that's whut! And before ye know it, everybody's cracking jokes about beanstalks and eggs and yev lost all o' yer respect!" The giant rose to his full height, blocking the sun behind him. "Oh, aye, they'd all love that, de bastards! They already pick on me 'cos ah'm short—just wait 'til they find out whut a big, friendly, and generous nature ah've got! Aye, I expect ah'll be takin kiddies back ta ma cave for lemonade and biscuits, yes?" Bregus took in a deep breath and lowered his face in front of the companions again. "NO!" he bellowed.

The force of the giant's breath knocked Xharon and Bip off their feet and sent them sprawling for several yards. Xharon gagged at the stench of raw meat.

"Now," continued the giant, "we all know how this goes—you trespass on my property, I eat you and then possibly turn you into bread-making utensils...though to be honest ah might give that last one a miss."

Bip, whose panicked brain had been searching manically for a plan, suddenly blurted something completely unexpected.

"I don't believe you!" he said.

The giant stared hard at him with eyes the size of wagon wheels. "Whut?" he said. "Would ye like ta repeat that?"

Bip swallowed hard and tried to keep his voice from shaking. "I don't believe you," he said. "I think you're all talk!"

His eyes not leaving Bip's face, Bregus casually raised his club and bought it down on a tree next to him, which buckled and fell to the clearing floor with an almighty crash. The Kaneqian tried hard not to break the giant's gaze. He was unsure of what part of his terror-addled brain this plan had come from, but he was determined to see it through.

"You know, you've got an awfy big mooth fer someone who doesn'e even reach me knee caps," growled the giant.

"Yes, well. It's just that I bumped into a group of chaps who reckon that you're just a big pansy, really."

Bregus's eyes narrowed. "Oh, aye? And who might that be?"

"A group of men we passed earlier on," said Bip. "We told them not to come down here, but they just said that…well…what was it they said? That they 'weren't afraid of some shorterse giant who couldn't fight sleep if he fell in a pot of coffee.'"

Bregus once more rose to his full height. "Whut!?" he roared.

"Yes," continued Bip. "And then they went on to say that…now what was it? Oh, yes! They said that you were 'uglier than a bugbear's behind and they were surprised you hadn't beaten yourself to death with your own stupid club.' Or something to that effect, anyway."

The giant said nothing, though his face went a deep, angry purple.

"And don't forget what they said about his mother," added Xharon, who had by now realized what direction Bip's plan was taking.

"Whut?" muttered Bregus through gritted teeth. "Whut did they say about my ma?"

"Only that she's so fat that she needs a map to find her bottom…"

Tears of rage began to flow from the giant's eyes. "Where are they?" he roared. "WHERE ARE THEY?!"

Wordlessly, Xharon and Bip pointed in the direction of the pathway they had come across. Bregus sprinted away from them, his footsteps thundering as he went. After a while, Bip stopped holding his breath, letting it out in a jet of relief. He turned to Xharon, who was looking at him with something close to admiration. "You know, you're cleverer than you look," she said.

Bip blushed and looked at the floor. It wasn't much of a compliment, but it would do.

ON THE CUSP OF HEARING, the thunder of horse hooves.

Handen opened his eyes, his mind carefully calm, his face devoid of any recognizable emotion. The time had come, and the adventurer was ready. He went through the motions, rechecking the weapons he had already double-checked, his mind reeling with the possibilities of attack and defense. It made no difference, he knew. In battle, the most carefully laid plans could be laid waste by a billion different factors, considered or otherwise. He knew that the only way to be truly ready was to be ready for anything.

The riders moved into view, the menace of their approach still softened by distance. Handen squinted and counted. Thirteen riders. He grinned. The pursuit had underestimated him, leaving behind a few men, probably to guard the provisions. It wasn't much of an advantage, but it was two fewer opponents than he had been anticipating and, small as it may be, the advantage was welcome.

The riders came nearer, the rumble of their horses' hooves increasing with every second. Handen surveyed his opponents one last time, and his breath caught in his throat. At the head of the pack, under a gray top-hat, a long greasy mane drew Handen's attention. He recognized Blungkit, the guard from the Bin, and instantly understood a few things about his pursuer. No nine-to-fiver was Blungkit. No bureaucrat or careerist. For Blungkit, this chase had been personal. Animal. And now Handen understood how he was tracked so well across a land as trackless as the Dozantyne Shrub.

The adventurer shook his head free of idle thoughts. The riders were approaching in the canyon below, and the time to act was almost upon him. Silently, he drew his pistola, checking that the powder was pressed correctly. Satisfied, he rested the weapon on his forearm and took careful aim at the advancing Regulators. They were coming exactly as he had hoped, slowing down sufficiently for the rough terrain, but too intent on the tracks of their quarry to suspect the ambush.

The Regulators advanced the only way the narrow canyon would allow them—two abreast and six long, with Blungkit in the lead.

Keeping the pistola rock-steady, Handen waited until the riders were nearly level with him and then, drawing a bead on the central Regulator, fired. The shot fired true, and the chaos was instantaneous. A horse, struck in the knee by the ballast of Handen's pistola, screeched horribly and tripped to the floor, throwing its rider, screaming, to the ground.

The narrow space and the speed of the Regulators ensured that panic descended swiftly, and the horses directly behind the fallen steed reared up over their comrade, one throwing its rider to the floor with an earth-shaking thump and the other dislodging a Regulator so that he hung helpless with his feet entangled in his stirrups.

The other Regulators managed to bring their mounts back under control and draw their pistols, searching the terrain around them for the threat. Blungkit recovered his senses first, barking orders for the men to form a circle and scan the trees. Handen allowed himself a grin. The shot was perfect, incapacitating three of the thirteen riders without even giving his position away.

Not wishing to give the Regulators time to recover from their shock, he leapt into the air and descended on them, drawing his bastard sword as he fell. By the time he hit the ground, he had already felled two of his opponents, striking a couple of unfortunate riders with the long-bladed sword as he landed.

One of the Regulators shouted a warning and aimed his flintlock at the ambusher. Without pausing for breath, Handen threw his now-useless pistola at the Regulator's head, knocking him out cold with the heavy steel grip.

The seven remaining Regulators, now fully aware of Handen's presence, aimed their pistolas and fired, unleashing a booming barrage of hot lead. The adventurer dived to the floor as the bullets began to fly, rolling across the ground and grabbing the fallen body of one of the recently dispatched Regulators. Using the body as cover,

Handen gritted his teeth at the sound of the rounded bullets impacting the flesh of his unfortunate shield. He reached around to the belt of the dead Regulator and drew a still loaded pistola. He fired a wild and unplanned shot, but a successful one. His target clutched at his shoulder, dropping his weapon as a pulse of blood spurted between his fingers.

Before Handen had time to register his good fortune, a bullet sliced through the calf of his exposed leg. Instinctively, the former Hostilities Advisor rolled backward and dived to the left, using one of the rider-less horses as cover. He looked at the wound on his leg. The pain was great, but he could still stand.

Blungkit, infuriated by the ambush, feverishly tried to reload his pistola. He looked up at his men and, seeing the idiot panic on their faces, roared in frustration. "Don't just stand there you useless idiots! Dismount and engage!"

Three of the riders dismounted, drawing their truncheons and handing their pistolas up to Blungkit's appointed wingman, Gordons, who began to reload the weapons. Blungkit looked at the fourth man, who was still clutching at his wounded shoulder.

"And what do you think you're doing?" he said. The wounded man turned to his leader with pleading eyes. Blungkit's fury redoubled. "Get down there and fight like a man, you maggot!" he bellowed.

The wounded man dismounted quickly and ran to join his comrades.

Coming out from his cover, Handen assessed his attackers. He knew that they were meant to slow him down, giving Blungkit time to reload and regain the firepower advantage. He would have to dispatch of them quickly if he wanted to maintain his aggressive momentum.

There were four of them, trained fighting men no doubt, but not in sufficient numbers to quell a man of a thousand years' combat experience. Plus, one of them was wounded, moving into the fray with obvious reluctance.

The four men circled the former Hostilities Advisor, their truncheons ready to strike. Suddenly, the wounded man gave a high-pitched cry and, truncheon raised to attack, ran at Handen.

The adventurer had time to almost feel sorry for his opponent who, in readying his weapon with his good arm, had left his wounded shoulder entirely open. Favoring his injured leg, Handen whipped a heavy back kick into the attacker's bleeding shoulder. There was a faint and stomach-churning squelching sound as boot connected with damp tissue. Instantly, the color left the attacker's face as a new fold of agony overwhelmed him. He sank to his knees, whimpering as the pain took the strength from his body.

Seeing an opening, the other Regulators attacked in a group. Handen rolled backward defensively and, with lightning speed, unfurled his whip, cracking it in an overhead circular motion and striking two of the attackers in the face. Bleeding and shocked, the Regulators stepped back, holding hands to their furiously stinging cheeks. Before they could get their footing, Handen ran in, pressing his advantage with a jumping front kick to the prone chin of the central Regulator. The man fell to the ground, teeth clenched and a faraway look in his eye.

Without hesitation, Handen raised his guard to his right, catching the descending wrist of another attacker and using his momentum to flip him onto the ground. The aggressor let out a loud *whoof* as the impact of the ground took the wind from his body.

Before Handon could regain his balance, a truncheon was brought down on his skull with an almighty thud. Handen, groggy and dazed, fell to his knees, his vision wobbling and swaying, only too aware of the Regulator coming from behind to finish him off. Fighting through his disorientation, he swung out a clumsy kick behind him that, by chance, connected with his assailant's groin. Handen winced and almost threw up as a sudden wave of pain reminded him not to kick with his wounded leg. Behind him, the Regulator crumpled to the ground, cross-eyed and mewling.

With all his opponents floored, either unconscious or in too much pain to move, Handen rose unsteadily to his feet and shook his head in an effort to clear the mugginess from his skull. He froze as something clicked loudly behind him.

Something that sounded exactly like the hammer being drawn back on a Regulator's pistola.

"I wouldn't move if I were you," came the gruff voice of Blungkit, and Handen felt the barrel of a flintlock pushed into the back of his head.

DARBY dug his stirrups into the flanks of his mare, forcing the horse into an even faster gallop. He smiled to himself. The trail was obvious, the prey drawing close. It was almost too easy.

The terrain under his mount had turned rocky, but so eager was Darby to catch up with his quarry that he barely registered the potential hazards. He sniffed at the air, almost tasting the tantalizing aroma of blood and promotion, when, without warning, his horse stopped dead, skidding to a complete halt with a hysterical whinny. Darby had just enough time to be annoyed by the sudden delay when he was thrown to the ground with bone-shaking force. Groaning, the Regulator got to his feet and turned to his men, who had all come to a halt behind him.

"Don't worry, I'm fine," he said. "Prepare to move out." Darby prepared to mount, and then stopped, puzzled. His men didn't appear to be listening to him, or even acknowledging his presence.

What could this be? Dissension in the ranks? Darby had waited for a long time for the chance at leadership, and he'd be damned if he'd lose the respect of his men just because he fell off his horse.

Darby drew in a breath, remembering all he had learnt from shadowing Blungkit these past weeks. "What are you waiting for, you scum? I said move!"

The other Regulators barely even registered that anything had been said. Darby began to sweat. Could he really be facing mutiny a mere couple of hours into his command?

"Oh, come on, lads," he said, reproachfully. "Play the game, eh? Fair's fair—I was put in charge, so I give the orders. So stop playing silly buggers and let's get a move on, shall we?"

The men still did not respond, merely stared ahead, their faces spookily blank. "What's going on?" said Darby, fear creeping into his voice.

Wordlessly, one of the Regulators raised a hand and pointed limply in front of him. Darby frowned and turned around. And then looked up. Blocking the sun was a bulky humanoid figure, stretching twenty feet and more into the sky.

Darby tried very hard not to spoil his uniform as a face like a full moon came level with his own.

"Ah heard ye've got something ta say ta me," said the giant, with a voice that resonates with sheer menace. Darby gulped, and the last thing he saw was the business end of a club that was really nothing more than a branchless tree.

EVEN ABOVE THE steady pounding of his horse's hooves, Bip could hear the distant cacophony of screams and crashes. Normally noises that would have made him cringe, today they filled him with an enormous sense of relief.

Rather them than me, he thought, and spurred his horse into a slightly faster run.

HANDEN EXHALED and raised his arms above his head. "Why don't you go ahead and shoot?" he said.

Blungkit barked a wet burp of laughter. "Not that easily, old son. We all know about you. Waste of a good bullet, shooting you."

"And what's that supposed to mean?"

"The Emperor told me all about you. Some kind of freak, you are. Can't be killed, or such like, so orders are to capture and detain indefinitely. Apparently, you are not to reach Argustin."

Handen's eyes widened in shock. How could anyone have known he was immortal? He hadn't told anyone but Bip and the others since he'd been incarcerated so many centuries ago. How could it be that the Emperor had found out?

"Yeah, the Emperor knows a lot about you, chum," said Blungkit, as if hearing Handen's thoughts. "You and your troublemaker friends."

Handen narrowed his eyes. "Well, if the Emperor knows so damned much, then how come he doesn't know about the meteor heading toward his planet, eh?"

Blungkit grinned his wet, wooden grin. "Who says he doesn't?"

Handen stood silently for a moment. When he spoke, his voice was a dark, flat calm. "Look, officer," he said. "I don't expect you to understand the amount of trouble I've gone through to warn the Emperor about this upcoming astral disaster, and I don't expect that you care, but let's imagine for a moment that you're right and the Emperor is fully aware of the crisis his world faces." Handen turned around slowly; Blungkit kept the pistol trained on his forehead. "Don't you think he'd want to talk to me? Find out what I know? See if I can help?"

Blungkit grinned. "Apparently not," he said. "Apparently he wants you to rot in jail."

The two men stood for a while. Handen felt himself tense for action. He doubted very much that he was quicker than Blungkit's trigger finger, and a bullet to the head, while it wouldn't kill him, could still put him out of action for a good few hours. He poised to attack and damn the consequences, then froze as a figure emerged behind the Regulator.

Blungkit didn't even look around. "Ah, Gordons," he said. "Do me a favor and clap this scum in irons, will you?"

There was no reply. Handen grinned.

"Gordons?" There was a sound like wood connecting with a coconut, and Blungkit's eyes crossed as though something terribly interesting had landed on his nose. "Guh?" he said, and crumpled to a heap on the floor.

"I thought you were staying with the horse?" said Handen.

Azron shrugged, hefting the truncheon in his hands. "I was curious," he said. He looked around at the heaps of gray-uniformed bodies, Regulators incapacitated in various ways. "Anyway, you seemed to be doing all right for yourself."

Handen shrugged modestly. In truth, he hadn't thought he would have been able to escape the posse, but fortune had been with him. He wasn't going to get complacent, however. "Let's get out of here before they come to their senses."

"Okay, just a sec," said Azron. The tall thief got to his knees and began patting the pockets of the unconscious Blungkit.

Handen gave a disapproving sigh. "Do we really have time for this?" he said.

"Just bear with me, okay?" said Azron. "I told you—I'm a thief! There's only one reason why a thief would knock someone unconscious and that's to steal from them. If I didn't at least take some of his personal possessions, then I'd be no better than a common thug, now would I?"

Handen shook his head in disbelief.

"And besides…" Azron held up a purse, which made a monetary chink when he shook it. "This might come in handy, don't you think?"

Handen couldn't suppress a wry grin. "Come on," he said. "We'd better catch up with the others and see if they're okay."

They made their way to their horse, leaving the conquered Regulators behind.

IT WAS NEARLY NIGHTFALL when Handen and Azron caught up with Bip and Xharon. There was a brief moment of explanation as each party told their respective tales, then a moment of spontaneous joy as the backwash of adrenaline heightened their senses, making them twice as glad to be alive and clearing their heads of panic with cool relief.

Handen was happy to let the backslapping and hand shakings go on, not even objecting when Bip suggested opening his bottle of Infamous Goose. By all accounts, the forces pursuing them had been badly crippled, and it would be some time before they recovered in sufficient numbers to pose a proper threat.

They camped that night, joking and retelling their stories in the warmth of the fire's glow, Bip nearly choking with laughter as Xharon recounted the giant's fury, and Azron giving a blow-by-blow account of what he had seen of Handen's fight with the Regulators.

Handen was happy to let them celebrate. Tomorrow the rush would wear off, and maybe then they would remember their fear and how close they had come to being killed or captured. But for now, with the cozy light of victory in their hearts, they could afford to laugh at death.

Handen laughed along, but not too loudly or too long. At the back of his mind, he kept thinking about an Emperor who claimed to be fully aware that the planet was in peril, yet still insisted on hunting down the people trying to warn him. It made no sense to the former Hostilities Advisor, and it worried him that the only way to get any answers would be to confront the man who would see them jailed, or worse, killed.

He lay back, looking at the stars and listening to the laughter of his friends. Tomorrow they would continue their quest, advancing into likely more treacherous territory, to explain themselves to a man who, by all accounts, had no interest in what they had to say. But tonight, under a canopy of gem-studded night, they could laugh like heroes.

***

SOMEWHERE IN THE DEEPER SHADOWS, Mr. Random fumed quietly. He could understand the failure of yetis and krakens and other dumb beasts—he could even understand the failure of the intellectually challenged giantkin he had drafted in as a precautionary measure— but the failure of Blungkit stung him deeply. He'd had high hopes for Blungkit and his men, and it annoyed him that they had been bested so easily.

The time was drawing near, and Random's plan had nearly reached its climax.

If he could just keep these troublemakers from interfering for a few weeks longer, then nothing would be able to stand in his way.

Either that, or he could speed things up a little.

The red-skinned being stroked his chin for a little while until a wicked grin appeared on his face. He snapped his fingers and disappeared with a pop.

***

BLUNGKIT AWOKE, the blurry mess before him eventually focusing into the concerned face of Gordons, looking down at him and framed in firelight against a darkened sky. A brief moment of perplexity gave way to angry realization. Blungkit scrambled to his feet, then immediately wished he hadn't. He put his hands on his knees and vomited a thin stream of bile onto the ground. Gordons took a few diplomatic steps backward.

"How long was I out?" said Blungkit, spitting the sharp taste from his mouth.

"A few hours, sir."

Blungkit cursed and gritted his wooden teeth. His head swam, and his guts felt unstable. He'd been concussed enough over his long career to recognize the symptoms. He turned to demand a roll call from his contingent, then stopped abruptly. Three of his men were laid out in a neat line with blankets over their faces. Many more were slouched about a campfire, alternately bruised and bandaged. Blungkit noticed the large, purple welt on Gordons's forehead.

"The bastards got the drop on us," he muttered. "Any news from Darby?"

Gordons shook his head. "We sent a scout to track him, sir. He found them. Sort of."

"Sort of?"

Gordons coughed. "They're dead, sir. Extremely dead."

"Extremely dead?"

"Perhaps the most extreme cases of death I've ever seen," said Gordons.

Blungkit nodded grimly. "Been in the job long, Gordons?"

"Seems that way, sir."

"I know how you feel."

The two men stood in silence for a while. When Gordons spoke, it was with obvious reluctance. "Are we continuing the pursuit, sir?"

Blungkit spat again. "Nah. No point. They've got at least a two-hour lead, and we've barely got a fighting man between us. We wouldn't stand a chance and, much as I think you lot are a useless shower of bastards, I'm not going to lead you to your deaths. Not today, anyway. We'll head back to Argustin and inform the Emperor that I've cocked up."

"He'll probably kill you though, sir," said Gordons, matter-of-factly.

"Yeah, I expect so, Gordons, I expect so." Blungkit scratched his chin thoughtfully. He was a Regulator to the core, and his loyalty and sense of duty forbade any other cause of action than returning to Argustin and accepting his punishment. Perhaps he'd be merely demoted, but he doubted it very much. So, he would return to the Empire and die the pointless and violent death he'd always assumed he would die.

Then he thought again, about the other man who was currently on his way to Argustin, the man who had taken on a squad of Regulators single-handed. If Blungkit was a gambling man, he'd bet that Handen Strike was heading to his certain defeat, but maybe…just maybe.

"Bury the dead and get the kettle on, lads. Tomorrow we head back to Argustin."

Blungkit sat down on the floor, putting his hands to the side of his throbbing head. He would head back to Argustin, but perhaps he would take the long way around.

UNDER A GENTLE AFTERNOON SKY, rustling peacefully in a cooling breeze, the garden was tranquil. The garden was always tranquil. In fact, Ted sometimes wondered if the garden was too tranquil. He gazed down at the perfect patch of soil he was working with his trowel and at the perfect vine of leaves that was already beginning to push its way up to the warm sunlight. Things grew easily in the garden, hardly needing any coaxing at all.

Just as an experiment, Ted envisioned a small gathering of slugs. They popped into existence, gray-coated and slimy, and began to munch immediately on the fresh leaves. Ted shook his head. Slugs, he knew, had their place in the world—for everything that grew, there had to be something that consumed—but seeing them here in his garden just seemed...wrong, somehow. He shook his head again, and the slugs faded from existence, sent back to wherever they had been summoned from.

Let the garden be tranquil. God knew you couldn't have enough peace and quiet in the ultraverse, and slugs were common enough.

For a while the gardener worked, digging gently at the soft soil and making rhythmical cutting sounds against the steady, pleasant bass of the wind. The sun shone perfectly, uninterrupted, and seemed it would do for the foreseeable eternity, until, without warning, a small cloud cast a shadow over the garden. Ted looked up from his digging, his eyes narrowing under his wiry gray brows. There had been a shift in the design, a tiny diversion from the way things were supposed to be going that, he sensed, could snowball into brand new inevitabilities. He sighed. Slugs in the garden.

Suddenly, with not so much as a blink of time passing, Ted was no longer in the garden, but floating through space.

By the way the stars and planets streaked past him, it appeared he was moving at incredible speeds, but Ted merely knelt, exactly as he was in the garden, trowel still in hand.

Beneath him, pacing him, like some dread undersea giant, a patch of darkness swam silently through the void, distinguishable from the surrounding space only by the way its mass consumed and excreted the hailstorm of stars that hurtled beneath it. Without appearing to move, Ted floated down closer to the object. From this perspective, we can see that the shape was nearly spherical, though bumpy and pointy here and there, with the occasional impression of nosecone or tail-fin, all thick and smothered with dust millennia old.

Ted was familiar with the Massive Ball of Death, just as he is familiar with everything in the ultraverse. He reached a hand down to the meteor-pocked surface of the moon-sized mass, feeling the metal and ice surface. He sensed the power in the cluster—enough to reduce Bersch to pebble-sized fragments—but he sensed something else, too. A consciousness was there, faint but undeniable. More a chaos of half-perceived yearnings than any sentient self-awareness, a sense of anticipation and direction that might have more in common with a flower turning toward sunlight. Ted was surprised by this, and also a little saddened. It was easy to feel sorry for any living thing this far from civilization and so close to inevitable oblivion.

After a subtle browse through of sub-matter frequencies, Ted was able to hear what the nuclear cluster was thinking…to a close approximation of thinking.

Nearly there. Nearly there. Nearly there.

Ted smiled. There was no loneliness or even malice in the Massive Ball of Death's consciousness—surprising for something born for nothing more than death and destruction. There was only an innocent sense of something resembling optimism.

With only a slight manipulation of subconscious wave patterns, Ted provoked an idea. The Massive Ball of Death shuddered slightly and then, at its rear, a long-dormant arming command suddenly sparked to life in long-dead control panels. There was a pause that shouted of ticking bombs, then a brilliant flash. The Massive Ball of Death leaked nuclear blast force from its rear like some inter-stellar guff and sped up, ever so slightly, toward its ultimate goal.

Nearly there. Nearly there. Nearly there.

Ted watched the incarnate disaster as it faded into the distance and smiled at a job well done. He is the Grand Design, the Final Blueprint. He is the be all and end all of everything, the inevitability of dramas uncountable, and of stories too vast to tell.

He knows that, above all, there has to be balance.

Without so much as a blink of time passing, Ted disappeared, leaving behind only stars and darkness.

BIP AWOKE from a night of bizarre dreams that teetered on the edge of his memory like a half-hearted suicide attempt. He had remembered a hazy theme, a brief and inexplicable feeling of falling that had ended as soon as it had begun, then a sensation that everything was somehow…not the same anymore.

The general feeling of unease was in no way helped by the discombobulating hangover he was suffering.

The night before had been cause for merriment, though after only a few drabs of Infamous Goose, the merriment had quickly accelerated into blind drunkenness. Mercifully, the party had passed out before they could do themselves any real damage. Bip's last memory was of laughing hysterically at Azron's impression of an irate duck—though the interrelated events had been lost to some mystifying void. Now Bip awoke, stiff from sleeping without his groundsheet and with the loose impression that seven kinds of woodland creature had crapped in his mouth.

He sat up, his lower back objecting heinously and his head seeming to swell and throb with the effort. Once again, Bip felt an odd sense of displacement. His body clock was telling him that it was nearing late morning, but the grainy quality of the light around him had more in common with twilight.

Surely they wouldn't have let me sleep in that long, thought Bip. He glanced around, slowly, so as to spare his suddenly loose-fitting brain, and saw his friends. They were all standing quite still and staring into the distance. Their lack of movement coupled with the eerie quality of the light had quite an unnerving effect, and for one mad moment, Bip became convinced that time had somehow stopped. He jumped to his feet, ignoring the dishwater feeling in his stomach, and ran over to his comrades and…stopped.

Hanging in the sky like a low flying star was...well...some sort of star by the look of it.

Flying low...

It hung there casually, as though it had never been anywhere else, droopy and glittery, the size of a thumbnail from this perspective, and shining with a kind of gray twinkle that put Bip in mind of a coin at the bottom of a wishing well.

"What is it?" he breathed.

Handen turned, as if shaken from a dream. "What do you think?" he said flatly.

Bip's eyes widened in sudden understanding. "It can't be," he said. "It can't be the astral disaster. We've months until it gets here, you said so yourself!"

"Apparently I was wrong," said Handen, turning back to the light in the sky.

The quartet watched for a long time, no one speaking.

"Blimey," said Xharon eventually.

"Yeah," agreed Azron. "I mean, I know you lot were on about the end of the world and stuff, but I didn't think you were serious!"

"Sort of brings the point home, really, doesn't it?" said Handen.

"Too right."

Bip brightened up a little. "Surely the Emperor will have to believe us now?"

"Not much of a consolation, Bip," said Handen. "Even if he does listen to us, we may be too late."

Xharon turned with a gasp, a look of heart-melting anxiety in her eyes that made Bip feel odd in his belly. "You're not giving up, are you?" she said.

Handen grinned. "Of course not. As long as we're alive, there's hope, and any help we can give to the Emperor could be vital. Besides, what else can we do?"

"Buy a really big umbrella?" muttered Azron.

Handen headed toward the horses, which were already packed and ready to go.

"We've two days until we reach Argustin," he said. "If we ride hard, we might make it there in one and a half."

He took the reins of his horse and cast one last glance to the sinking star, hanging there with all the promise of a billion deaths.

"Let's move."

AND HERE IS as good a place as any to leave, as villains lick their wounds and heroes gallop across the plains, racing against time to an uncertain fate. And so we will leave the people of Bersch as they awaken to a dawn sky quite different from any they have seen before. For now, let them exclaim in wonder and curiosity at the new daytime star that lights the sky, because soon, very soon, they are going to learn that wonder and curiosity are the bastard sons of horror.

This is the planet Bersch, spinning endlessly on its axis as it has done since time immemorial. This is the planet Bersch, lit from a new perspective by a galactic intruder. This is the planet Bersch, and it may be spinning out its final days…

To Be Continued in *The Mad Emperor*
Book 3 of The Doomsayer Journeys
Available Now from Falstaff Books

If you enjoyed this book and would like to be notified of new releases, appearances, and everything else related to Steve Wetherell, sign up for the newsletter here -
http://eepurl.com/cv5FSj

Acknowledgments

Special thanks to Rebecca Hill for editing the initial publication of this book, and to Graham White for the original cover art.

About the Author

Steve Wetherell is an author, comedy writer and podcast idiot. He regularly writes humorous nonsense on the internet, and cordially invites you to join him. He lives in the English midlands with his wife, kids, and laptop, and his interests include beer, rock music and writing about himself in the third person.

Also by Steve Wetherell

Authors & Dragons - Podcast

Hell's Titties

The Totally Legend of Brandon Thighmaster

The Ballad of Aaron Bezron

Shoot the Dead

Far into the Dark

The Torso Farmer

Falstaff Books

**Want to know what's new
And coming soon from
Falstaff Books?**

Try This Free Ebook Sampler

https://www.instafreebie.com/free/bsZnl

**Follow the link.
Download the file.
Transfer to your e-reader, phone, tablet, watch, computer,
whatever.
Enjoy.**